Witches Brew

Witches Brew

The Whitborough Novels

Alistair Lavers

Matador
9 Priory Business Park,
Wistow Road, Kibworth Beauchamp,
Leicestershire, LE8 0RX
Tel: 0116 279 2299
Email: books@troubador.co.uk
Web: www.troubador.co.uk/matador
Twitter: @matadorbooks

ISBN 978 1789015 805

British Library Cataloguing in Publication Data.
A catalogue record for this book is available from the British Library.

Printed and bound in the UK by TJ International, Padstow, Cornwall
Typeset in 11pt Aldine401 BT by Troubador Publishing Ltd, Leicester, UK

Matador is an imprint of Troubador Publishing Ltd

Dedicated to The Damned

Contents

A Paean to Yorkshire

'Yer not frum round 'ere... arrr yer?'

What is magnificent and beautiful in England that Yorkshire does not also possess?

Yorkshire, land of shivering cricket teams and the biggest chip on the shoulder of northern England. A land of upturned collars and mud-covered tyres – where small dogs snarl and women lurk in ambush.

Yorkshire, land of enigmatic misty moors, vast rolling hills, sprung with ankle-breaking heather, solitary, defiant trees, bent and crippled by howling gales – and sports cars in ditches.

Yorkshire, the cradle of the Yorkshire Dales, as pretty, characterful and lush as any of Kent and Dorset's rural idylls, even beneath the sheeting rain; and on the coast Whitby, Whitborough, Filey, Scarborough and Runswick Bay, the equals of any seaside towns in Devon and Cornwall – but with gusting wind and litter.

Yorkshire, the county born of York and Yorkists, with more history and culture than Edinburgh and Glastonbury combined and a hundred types of ale to guarantee you miss your train.

Yorkshire, the home of Leeds – and a ring road of such fiendish wickedness that it rivals London's famous Hanger

Lane Gyratory for turning placid drivers into potential mass murderers.

Yorkshire, the mother of Beverley which has one of the most architecturally beautiful main avenues outside of Bath, and a market square to cheer the grumpiest historian. And a pie shop for every bank.

If ever a citizen of the world desired to see all of England condensed – with an even chance of survival – they could do no better than to spend their time in this most wonderful, yet puzzling, locality. Some minor financial losses and a constant feeling that one is being "looked up and down" are a small price to pay for the majestic scenery; and a visit to Yorkshire is never truly complete without at least two or three instances of provocative questioning from one of the natives, usually punctuated by awkward, but deeply meaningful, silences. If one is able to tolerate these small peculiarities and not take the blunt, gruff or taciturn behaviour of the natives too personally, the experience can only have a positive impact on one's learning and strength of character; and the departing guest will be eternally grateful to the men and women of Yorkshire, for putting them right.

Precursor.

It is to Yorkshire now – and Britain's first resort, the perpetually hazardous Whitborough on Sea – to which we return inside these pages – ignoring the occasional mysterious spots of blood that may blot the text from time to time, and the faint smell of burning – to discover the grisly, yet paradoxically amusing fates of those whose lives have been forever marked after handling the infamous and deadly Treasure of the Mar del Norte. A treasure with two fatal curses on its shoulders. 'A treasure that nobody in their right mind would want to find', wrote Archbishop Theo Bann-Bolding, the chairman of Parliament's reparations tribunal, in his summing up of the investigation into its disappearance, two full years after the end of the English Civil War.

The treasure's peaceful interment, in the clay soil of Cayton Bay's cliff top plateau, came to an end in the second chapter of *Treasure Trove* when a local solicitor, Derek Beautimann, and his legal secretary, Maureen Moment – the most senior figures of Whitborough's accident-prone Black Hand Coven – returned to the scene of their previous night's ritual with spades and shovels, and two large sports holdalls, to dig for old bones and the promise of gold. One night and several fly bites after the exact location had been revealed to them by the corresponding supernatural authority; a balloon-sized globe of pus, rancid saliva and snake venom, by the name of Tetarzepamdomestoz, which had later escaped the plateau above Cayton Bay before the coven's banishing ritual could be performed and is, at this very moment, re-constituting itself from dead pigeons, legionnaire's bacteria and silverfish corpses in a derelict water tank under the dusty attic timbers of the Dickens Hotel, readying itself for another assault on the collective continence of Whitborough's tourist industry after instigating an Easter plague which emptied nearly every supermarket and small shop in the borough of Andrex, Sudocrem and Dettol.

In addition to the Easter plague, there had also been four severe incidences of what could only be described as either terrorism or violent sabotage by a foreign power. *HMS Heddon,* the town's adopted ship, had been destroyed by a junior sixth form history teacher, whose expertise with Civil War era artillery had surpassed any war historian's theoretical knowledge by a lucky first hit and thirty years at Her Majesty's pleasure at Wold Newton Prison.

Two police vehicles and a BMW R100RT police bike had also been destroyed at Carr Wold Parkway – by machine gun fire. Another police car had been turned to scrap by a rocket launcher in the Whitborough to Bridlington railway tunnel. And four coastguard stations had been torched. All of these "small" catastrophes were preceded by the "surprise" discovery of a 55kg Luftwaffe air bomb in the flowerbeds beside the southerly supporting pillars of Valley Bridge on Kenwith Valley Gorge, the great road bridge connecting Lower Gunstone to the town centre.

Landkey Island, four miles offshore, survived all the excitement unscathed. It had often avoided the violent events that shaped the fate of its adopted town on the mainland. Landkey's community was presently comprised of forty-two hardy souls and several small businesses – Brodie's General Store and Post Office, Brodie's Newsagent and Gift Shop, Cribbs Hotel and Cafe, Scrapes the Grocer's, McGuigans the Baker, Patterson's Fish and Chip Shop and the Briny Ewe Inn; all squeezed in a tight huddle around the small harbour on the landward side of the island, where the worst of the prevailing wind and rain is only vindictive, rather than deliberately murderous.

Landkey, three miles wide and ten miles long, is aligned along a north–south axis corresponding to 135 degrees north, to the northeast of Whitborough Castle. The island is steepest on its seaward side, with a central plain of small green fields lined with rock walls in the same pattern as the ancient field systems of the Outer Hebrides. The edge of the island is ringed by woodland. It has many stone circles, burial mounds and the remains of a Stone Age settlement, Skara Broc. There is also a small wooden chapel, in the Norwegian style, with a shingle roof, a lighthouse and a rather bleak castellated house, called Weareburgh, on a large wooded plot surrounded by a high wall. It has only four occupants – the sorceress, Sveta Alexandra Anchabadze, the former paramour of Derek Beautimann, and her servants, the Stapletons.

Sveta, a long-standing resident of Landkey, had been born a refugee in the chaos of war in Königsberg, Eastern Prussia in 1945. Her family, the last survivors of the aristocratic Russian Anchabadzes, eventually reached Denmark and secured safe passage to England and Weareburgh, an island estate which the family had purchased as a sanctuary with the last of their assets just before the outbreak of World War Two. Sveta was blessed with the gift of second sight and a natural aptitude for communicating with the spirit world. She was also a practised herbalist and observer of nature. Weareburgh was her home and her paradise, and since arriving as a young girl she had never left.

Chapter One

Hunter's Moon.

A half-veiled, milky full moon cast down its deathly glow over the farmsteads and sporadic huddles of rustic cottages along the great coastal valley of Kettleness, five miles north of Whitby. At Valley End, in front of the estuary, the last church bell rang out as the earth turned under the constellations. By ten o'clock, the small scattered flecks of light from the mosaic of rambling dwellings began to go out, until nothing but the bright pinpricks of the stars remained to offset the corpse-like pallor of the moonlit scene.

Kettleness, the oldest inhabited valley in the British Isles, had once been part of the great Anglo-Saxon kingdom of Mercia, and was later absorbed into the outlying estates administered by Whitby Abbey under William the Conqueror. When England had been partitioned into counties, it had become part of the great county of North Yorkshire. But Kettleness had always had its own unique character – and a reputation as a place unlike any other. A place where "unnatural" things happened. A place where people suddenly vanished, never to return. Kettleness was cursed. Kettleness was werewolf country.

The wolf spell curse had entered the bloodlines of the native "Kettlers" with the northern tribes from across the

Viking ocean, after the withdrawal of the last Roman legions – though witches had also been part of its community for as long as the land had been worked by human hands. Resting on the confluence of four major ley lines, the rocks and soil of Kettleness had endured three millennia of ritual magic and invocation, thinning the veil between the world of men and sheep and the world of ghosts and otherworldly forces to such a degree that the supernatural kingdoms often encroached or overlapped upon the physical. In the stagnant mists of its darkest hollows, where the dead and the living walked in step, it was a brave act indeed to be out alone without the precaution of company – especially at one particular time of the month.

Although the lower valley was unofficially "off limits" during the hours of darkness for lone walkers, life went on much as normal for the residents of Kettleness during the hours of daylight. People had to make a living, fences had to be mended and dogs had to be walked – whether they wanted to tiptoe in the same tracks as enormous supernatural predators or not.

For the rapscallion hardcore of native Kettlers, whose lives were still anchored firmly in the physical world, life in the valley had always been a trial. The high, windswept ridges of Chappell Heights and South Heights – and the bright green fields quilting the long drop to the torpid stream that ran from Hocum Cauldron, through its mystical heart in Blasteene Wood and Dolmen Pool – required much hard work and patience for only moderate rewards. The once rich jet mine, and the famous gold seam that ran below it, had long since ceased to support any serious prospecting, and were now nothing more than derelict curiosities that occasionally blessed the more determined amateur miners. But the mines were now dark and dangerous places for the unwary. The valley was now little more than a collection of farms, and a dormitory settlement for those residents of Whitby who could afford to maintain an old house with land.

Kettleness – in the words of its most famous resident – Angus Charles Chappell – inventor of the two-stage distress flare rocket and the broom-roller sheep dip – had endured "twelve bloody Chappell graves too long". Though for anyone of means who enjoyed spectacular scenery, fresh air and solitude, it was heaven on earth.

It is here, halfway down the north ridge of Chappell Heights, inside the lounge partition of a large static caravan, that we rejoin our unlikely hero, Dudley Kingcombe, of Beere Farm, Washbum Pomeroy, and his host Conrad "Conn" Thatcher, of Harker Farm, Kettleness, just before midnight on a spring evening in the year 1983, as the first regiments of snowdrops and daffodils have opened their bright bonnets.

Dudley, the deadliest hunter in Devon, despite a pair of knees that were farther apart than the towers of Clifton suspension bridge, and a pair of arms that had come direct from the prosthetic appendages workshop for *Planet of the Apes*, would have gone all the way to the top as a physical comedian in a big city, had fate not set him down as a farmer's son in the green hills above Honiton, in rural Devon. But Dudley was content. Happy maintaining his family's farm, happy delivering body bags to the hill farms of Devon and Cornwall, and happy to tease the heretical cliques in the Department of Agriculture and Rural Affairs with the occasional muddy plaster cast of a puma's paw and the kind of feral turd that gets zoological students and geneticists very excited.

Few of Dudley's contemporaries told a joke at Dudley's expense anymore; apart from the small group of divorcees that he nimbly avoided in the course of his weekly shop in Norman's Supermarket in Honiton. But Dudley didn't worry too much about finding a partner – he was his own man and was rather suspicious about the motivations of the opposite sex – being half ape, half gargoyle. But at least he did not have to worry too much about money. He was now one of a select group of "covert" contractors – for four county councils from Wiltshire to Cornwall – with a hitlist to rival a Sicilian mafioso's year planner; dispatching the kind of predatory felines that no-one in their right mind would have sitting on their lap.

Dudley had arrived in Kettleness some hours before in his olive green ex-army Bedford truck, hauling enough firepower to drop anything up to and including a fully grown grizzly bear, with a mission to find and kill a mysterious predator that had recently arrived in the locality. A predator with an appetite that was as random and rapacious as it was shocking.

The mysterious creature had already savaged some valuable rams at Harker Farm, and had cleared out every fox and badger in its range, prior to making inroads into the smaller livestock populations on the many smallholdings within the district. Its biggest mistake had been its attack on a very spoiled pet cat by the name of Marmalade, a gluttonous lap warmer and slipper thief, belonging to Whitby town councillors, Bryn and Mavis Halshaw – prominent members on Whitby Council's leading committees through five Prime Ministers.

Marmalade's devoted mummy and daddy were not going to take his grisly demise lying down, unlike the remaining rear end of their precious pet that had been chomped back to his ribs. But the Halshaw's quest to assemble a team to orchestrate the hunt for his killer had taken much time and effort behind the scenes – and time was not on their side. The recent disappearance of two campers from Ash Gill Ravine, behind Blasteene Wood, had added extra impetus and urgency to the appointment of a competent hunter and tracker. But sadly, despite all the clues, only a handful of natives still knew that the valley and its borders were not "*as other places*". Now, to add to all its other problems – and restless spirits – Kettleness had a headless phantom cat.

Conrad Thatcher and Dudley Kingcombe, however, were not known for speculating or ruminating deeply upon the nature of reality or the supernatural. Both men were farmers, both were tough, economical with words and reliably single-minded; shaped by duties and responsibilities that could not be shirked or postponed, duties that moulded men into doers, rather than philosophers. Theirs was an odd and potentially awkward partnership, but they had recognised in each other a kinship, born out of the mutual experience of hard work in all weathers, not often experienced outside the farming community. It was this *esprit de crops t*hat had, thus far, carried them through their communication difficulties in their business arrangement – as coming from opposite ends of the country, it was a minor miracle that they could understand each other at all.

The two men had just carried the last of Dudley's equipment from his Bedford into the caravan and were getting ready to part company after exchanging a few final pleasantries.

'So that's for thee, Dudley,' said Conn, setting down a Yale key on the table of the static caravan at which his guest was seated in front of his rifle. 'Use that instead o' the padlock ont door from now on. I thought I'd lost that bloody key 'til it turned up in one o' me baccy tins. Alluz got more than me one tin ont go – only bloody pleasure I've got left,' he grunted, 'nice little bolt hole this caravan – all the comforts of 'ome wee-out the stress… If there's owt else y'need – you know where we are. There's a standpipe tap outside ont concrete where y'can wash yer boots; thuzz electric an' gas, but yull need tee come up tee us at farm for owt else. If ya need ta call us there's a walkie-talkie wee new battrees in the 'ead locker above the sink, cos there's no phone line down 'ere. I carry t'other one – on me belt. Nearest proper call box is ont t'other side at boundary next t'chapel on Lazy Jane Lane. The radios are fine out t'boundary… about 1000 yards.'

'This'll do me well enough, Mr Thatcher.'

'Call me Conn.'

'Conn it is then… You got a pub round yerr?'

'The Rowan Tree's nearest… bit of a walk.'

'Oh yeah?'

'Two mile down Lazy Jane Lane, overt' big gate,' he said, nodding in the direction of the lower field. 'I'd get yer sen a taxi back, unless you're training for a shot at hiking up Snowdon or Ben Nevis,' said Thatcher, alluding to the near vertical nature of the main lane down to the valley. 'Fish 'n' chips are okay. Shepherd's Pie's all right too. All day breakfust's a bit middling. Fust 'alf o the week.'

'Middling?'

'Aye, that's polite – for shite. If weekend chef's on you'll be reet. Monday, Tuesday, Wednesday or Thursday I wouldn't eat the bloody food if it were free; I don't know what that young 'un who cooks forrem does tutt fried bread an' 'ash browns. Grits 'em wee rock salt I shouldn't bloody wonder. Last bacon rashers they gev me… looked like they'd bin tipped in a pressure cooker then finished off wee a blow torch. A word o' warning though – if you're game enough ta walk back and hear a car coming, mek sure you get y'sen off the road an' ont verge sharpish. There's some reet mad bastards roaring up an' down Lazy Jane after hours; local clowns, practising futt rally at Dalby. We've 'ad quite a few of 'em go off grass tracking, over the years. That's what's medd all them bloody great gaps in us 'edges. I charge our crashers two 'undred quid a time to pull 'em out weet' tractor. Then the daft buggers go and do it again a week later. Still, keeps us in beer an' fags and a few mini-breaks at Christmas.'

'Thanks for the warning. You going that way?'

'Aye, fancy a pint before you start?'

'Sounds good to me.'

'Might be best if I tek yer in and introduce ya, before I clear off. Some o' the Rowan Tree regulars can be a bit funny wee strangers. A bit like the bloody staff…'

'Sounds loike Northern Ireland.'

'You seen a bit o' trouble then, Dudley?'

'Bout average, jus' the usual gunfoights. It'll be a damn noice place to take a caravan – when the sods stop killing each other.'

'Never bin ta Ireland.'

'If you thought England wuz wet, wait till you gets across the Irish Sea. Moind you, all the bleddy rain 'elps put the fires an' the petrol bombs out.'

'I think I'll stick ta Yorkshire. While you're 'ere, we'll keep bottom pasture 'ere free fo' thee, an' try an' stay out yer way – best we can. Me an' me lads 'ull tek the Jersies inside at dusk. The lambs an' the yews'll be in t'barn. So you'll not 'ave to worry about shooting owt that shouldn't be shot at. Nice looking rifle you got there. Can't say I've ever used a rifle. Always had shotguns – over an' unders. I don't rate side bee side shotguns; you don't want another barrel blocking your eye line when you're following a moving target out 'ere. All right fut gentry; it's not life or death if them buggers miss owt. Most o' the twats couldn't hit a bullock with an artillery battery.'

'Ha! Same story down the Taunton valley. I once 'ad a mind to take out city types on hunting trips. First group we did – me an' Pa – one o' these twerps shot his mate in the arse when we was on stag. You can't imagine all the bloody paperwork I 'ad to fell in fer Norwich Union. Took all the pleasure out o' shooting yer guests,' he chuckled. 'This yerr theng's a Remington 700, Conn, best bleddy rifle money can buy – see, that's what I reckon anyways; we got shotguns too; but you need a good rifle for this kinda work; sometimes you only gets to put these things down from a ways off. Too close an' they smell eee comin if the winds aren't right. Where's these dogs o' yours to on a night? Theym indoors?' asked Dudley, patting Conn's collies, Shepp and Dora.

'Aye, they're in wee us. They've got their own beds int boot room. Owt else you wanna know before we set off?'

'Nope, that's champion.'

'Well, be lucky while you're 'ere.'

'No luck involved,' said Dudley, patting his rifle cover. 'If the bastard's in range eez as good as skinned for a rug. Don't expect to see anything tonight though. Other things to do first. Foind a place ta set up a hide that's in just the right place after dark. Somewhere the wind don't blow too 'ard, a noice theck copse between high and low ground overlooken' a bend on that stream.'

'Right, if you got somewhere to put that we'll get going,' said Conn, nodding at Dudley's rifle before offering some more words of wisdom. 'I'll not say t'much about this thing Dudley. But ya best watch y'sen. It's a nasty piece o' work.'

'Oi didn't loike to say so afore, being the polite sort,' he said, smirking slightly. 'But oi getz a sense there's sumthen a wee bett unusual wi' this yerr gig... Scuze me for being blunt...'

'Just mek sure you don't miss,' muttered his host as he stepped out of the caravan.

'Don't often miss. You know... I'll tell eee summin... jus' fer reference... a tiger, your average tiger... theym only got thirty teeth, roughly speaken' – that's what eez born weth. Dogs, on the other hand, see – diffrent again. Most o'they got forty-two...'

'And?'

'Intrestin, innett? The things you can foind out... if you start diggen. The only reason oi mentions it now, see – is cuz oim a bit curious to know 'ow many teeth this bugger o' yours 'uzz got. The picture o' that ram o' yours your copper fella Jackson sent me ain't no big cat kill. Looked more loike a bloody shark attack. A fella like me, see, moight be a bit curious to know what kinda thengs you got running about up yerr that like taking such gert begg chunks o' meat outta stuff.'

'Well, all I'll say is, it ain't no tiger. Just tek my advice an' tek yer pistol with ya an all – sorry about the state of the pickup,' added his host diffidently, brushing some cattle feed pellet dust off the scarred vinyl passenger seat.

'No worries, oi sat on worse in the army.'

9

Ten minutes later the two men stepped out of Thatcher's Toyota pick-up in front of the ivy-covered front wall of the Rowan Tree, at the bottom of Lazy Jane Lane, and walked inside, taking a sharp right turn inside the front door to the public bar.

'I'll 'ave a pint o' Tetley's, Flo,' said Conn to the barman, 'what'll it be, Dudley?'

'Pint o' Stowford Press for me please,' replied Dudley, 'thanks very much… will ya be alroight for droiving?'

'The law's a bit more elastic out 'ere. We don't bother them, if they don't bother us. Ain't that right, Flo?'

'Huh! It's lucky for them that we haven't got the breathalysers the way they put it away. Who's your friend?'

'This is Dudley,' said Conn, cocking his head towards Dudley. 'Dudley – this is Flo. Flo's… been 'ere a while,' said Thatcher, resisting the temptation to expound.

'Flo…' said Dudley, curbing the temptation to ask the slightly chubby barman in the pink shirt anything impertinent.

'It's short for Florence, honey.'

'Dudley's from down south, Flo.'

'Oh… nice… Dorset?'

'Devon.'

'And what do you do, sweetpea?'

'*Pest control…*'

'Oh. Please yourself…'

'Don't mind Flo, Dudley. He's just a bit camp.'

'You've got a nerve, Conrad Thatcher.'

'Dudley's doing some work for us. A bit of trapping…' added Conn, clearing his throat. 'Dudley's gonna need a taxi, Flo.'

'Hold yerr 'orses, Conn, oi don't drink that fast,' chuckled the Devonian.

'If yer wanting a lift later, best order it now, that's all. Taxis are a bit slow round 'ere. I've never met any bugger else that drives for a living who thinks ten minutes means owt between thirty an' sixty. Eh, Flo?'

'You're not wrong there.'

'Ain't you got no other taxi companies up yerr then?'

'Nope, just the one. One controller, four drivers.'

'One piss-artist,' added the wrinkled old countryman two stools away by the door.

'Don't you go scaring my guest, Jack – you old bugger,' joked Conn, cracking a smile.

'Well, that's me,' said Conn, draining his glass. 'I'll leave you in the capable hands of Flo and Jack here.'

'You not staying for another then?'

'Not tonight, Dudley... I just remembered I got some work of my own to do. I'll see you in the morning. You can stand me a pint next time.'

'Sees you in the mornen then, thanks for helping me with me gear. What's this yerr taxi company called?'

'Beehive. Safe to say they'll *bee* bloody late.'

'I'll bear that in moind then.'

'You're welcome. Flo can fix you up. Flo takes care of business, don't you, Flo?'

'You don't say,' added Dudley – under his breath.

'What's that, dear?' asked the barman.

'Think oim about ten minutes frum needing a taxi, friend...' replied Dudley, licking his lips. 'However long ten minutes ezz round yerr.'

Chapter Two

The Supernatural Caravan Club.

A few miles away, inside another static caravan in a screened field above Runswick Bay, Dudley's prime target, Lindsay Boldwood, landlord of the Shirestones Hotel in Cloughton village, and Mother Nature's largest ever lycanthrope, was getting himself ready for bed on his first night away from his hotel for as long as he could remember. Though his temporary absence was more of a breathing space, rather than a proper holiday, an opportunity to discover more about the pattern and possible cause of his mysterious seizures, far away from the eyes of his friends and neighbours.

Boldwood had just begun to relax and adjust to his new surroundings, with a bottle of Talisker and a copy of *The Cruel Sea,* when he felt the first tell-tale signs of another imminent swoon as he drew up the zip of his sleeping bag. Knowing that he probably only had a few more seconds of consciousness before the darkness came upon him, he managed to reach out and press record on the small dictation machine beside his cot and hurl a couple of Anadin Plus tablets past his moustache and beard before he started to succumb to the terrible effects of the ancient lycanthrope virus, as it charged into his bloodstream from the tiny gland behind his eyes. The sleeping bag constraining the fainting

12

publican now began to bounce and squirm on the cabin bed base boards like an otter having a panic attack inside a Christmas stocking, as the changeling's emerging claws began to tear and shred the lining from the inside out, until the whole of the bedroom compartment was choked with goose feathers and a snowstorm of thermal wadding. The bed boards under the thin foam mat now began to rattle in tune with his fitting, as his transformation moved towards its climax, adding another discordant racket to the brutal squeaking from the stainless steel brackets and rails holding the bed's box-frame to the caravan's steel chassis. As the tubby publican began his unconscious metamorphosis into a gigantic carnivorous killer, a hairy elbow burst through the right seam of the bag, shearing off the plastic window catch, then his emerging hind feet tore through the bottom of his sleeping bag, tipping him off the hard edge of the chipboard box-frame onto the strip of carpet tiles where he broke his whisky tumbler with the hairy edge of his eye socket and was soon being uncomfortably squeezed around the shoulders between the bed frame and the caravan wardrobe as his new form expanded with grim rapidity, asserting his shaggy bulk against the wardrobe door and the lower bed panels.

'That fella that moved into number four yesterday seems to be having a right old fight with something,' muttered Boldwood's neighbour, Carol Timms, to her husband, Jim, as they sat in bed reading not twenty feet from the largest, greediest werewolf in the history of the breed panting inside the caravan next door.

'How's your book, Jim?'

'Can't hear anything now,' observed her husband, commenting on the abrupt lull in Boldwood's exertions.

'He might need some help – do you think we should check he's all right?'

'Carol, I'm not going outside now in my bed shorts and t-shirt to speak to someone I've only met once for a few seconds two days ago. Especially if he's only come here to bounce up and down on his secretary.'

'Where's he got a woman from, this time of night?'

'Anywhere that's big enough to have a bus stop, I should think.'

'Don't be facetious – you know what I mean... I get the feeling I've met him somewhere before. I just can't remember where... and don't you get any ideas,' she added.

'We wouldn't have to listen to his bloody exertions if you'd keep that bloody window shut.'

'I like having it open. I like me fresh air... God knows we need some with your squeaking backside growling all night. Did you catch his name?'

'No – *and I didn't ask.* People come here for a bit of peace and quiet – and privacy.'

'Well I hope he won't be bashing into things all night. I can't be sleeping with the window shut. It's not natural.'

'Looks like you'll have to put up with a bit of extra noise then won't you – *and* that bloody moth you've let in,' groaned Mr Timms, looking at the giddy insect that was hypnotically headbutting the light bulb with a psychotic enjoyment out of all proportion to any obvious reward.

'Just shoo it out with the paper.'

'*You* shoo it out – *you* let the bloody thing in.'

'I haven't got me slippers. They're in the lounge. And I'm not setting my feet down on the floor, it's cold.'

'Oh for God's sake...' muttered Mr Timms, 'turn

14

the light out – while I get the damn thing out the door.'
Mr Timms swung his legs out of bed and felt for his own
slippers, picking up his dressing gown as he shuffled toward
the bedroom door. 'Draw those curtains, Carol, we're not
letting in all its bloody mates when I switch the lights on
again.'

'Are you going to check on that fella next door?'

'*No, I'm not.* His private shagging habits are of no interest
to me whatsoever.'

Boldwood climbed up onto his bed and sniffed the air
outside through the gap in the window and then pushed the
glass out with his nose. The window aperture was a little tight
but eventually he managed to squeeze his way through and
flopped down on the line of concrete paving stones laid around
the caravan's base. A fox suddenly appeared at the top of the
tree-break between the caravans and stopped to stare at him,
until it suddenly decided it was probably in its best interests
to get out of the immediate area as fast as possible. Boldwood
decided to follow its scent and see if it led him towards any
promising kinds of prey. As he reached the spot where the fox
had appeared, the door of the caravan on the opposite side to
Mr and Mrs Timms opened, illuminating a small rectangle of
grass beyond. Boldwood hesitated on the farthest edge of the
illuminated ground then moved forward into the light. His
other neighbour, Bruce Butcher – a middle-aged DJ, stepped
down from the doorway, casting a long shadow, and opened
the lid of a dustbin a few feet beyond the door and scraped
the remains of his tea into the bin before replacing the lid
and returning to his caravan. Boldwood moved forward and
growled. The man turned around, peered into the burning
yellow eyes of the meanest, fattest predator he had ever seen

since Fay Wray swooned into the sweaty palm of King Kong in Cleethorpes Odeon, and ran back inside as fast as was humanly possible for a man wearing flip flops and sarong.

Chapter Three

A Fortune, a Fire, a Wolf at the Door.
One Stray Bullet Wrecks a House.

Twenty-five miles away to the south, another drama of supernatural origin was unfolding in the lair of former Aberdeen gangster, Barnett Crosbie, manager of Mystery City and the current apex predator of Whitborough on Sea, as he opened the exit door of his attic flat in his nightclub and stood quietly on the small box landing at the top of the staircase sniffing the air. Barnett's nose had just alerted him to the weak scent of smoke inside the tunnel-like staircase void leading up to his attic flat door, but no accompanying sounds or activity from the lower floors was yet forthcoming. After listening quietly for another minute he crept quietly down to the next level of the building, still clasping the machete he kept inside his pillow case, then opened the fire door onto the first landing and carefully approached his office door. He paused again, now aware of a stronger smell of burning wood below, then hastily slid back the metal link concertina doors to the former lift cage that now served as his office, approached the front screen to the spot where he had the best view of the dance floor below and then threw the main light switch.

It was immediately obvious that something was ablaze as the whole dance floor below was obscured by a grey fog which was certainly not the same smoke as the ground-hugging smog pumped out by the smoke machine. The smoke seemed to be thickest around the DJ's island so Barnett decided to get downstairs as fast as he could to throw open the front and rear fire doors and clear the smoke so he could better locate the source and put out the fire without having to involve the fire brigade.

When both sets of fire doors were open he ran back up to the first floor, while the smoke was clearing, and woke his friend and minder inside the projector room by kicking away the chair he was balanced on, dumping his partner in crime on the floor.

'Sheft yersell, Jamesy! Thurrs smoke on the stairs!'

'OWWW! Dedd yee have tae keck my arse off ma chair ya c★★t!'

'Aye I dedd!'

'You're no focking right enn the heyd – you!'

'No, I'm no'. An neither are yoo ya c★★t – now sheft yersell – I said the club's orn fire!'

'FIRE! Ya kedden!'

'Ahm no' kedden ya daft c★★t! Thurrs focken smoke cummen oot the DJ's island – get th' black CO2 extinguishers an' meet us doonstairs! An' dinnae crack the thengs on the wolls – y'ken?'

★

Back on the caravan park above Runswick Bay, Boldwood the Werewolf was investigating the warm scents floating out of his neighbour's galvanised steel dustbin, pausing to collect more scent molecules with his great wet nose – weighing up percentages. Whilst the terrified tenant he had taken by surprise looked on in horror and fascination through a chink in the blind behind his window, unsure whether taking a picture of this most frightening of beasts would provoke an attack on his fragile shelter. He decided to take the chance and lined up his compact 110 camera, then carefully pressed the shutter key, taking care to hold a dark serviette over the flash to avoid any unwanted attention from the monster on his bin. The odours from the corpse of the half-eaten meat feast pizza were almost irresistible to Boldwood, but the pong of chili-infused virgin olive oil and garlic were just too much even for his adventurous palate. Though like all members of the canine family tree he refused to pass over any scent of food traces without adding some of his own bodily fluids as territorial marker, and so he cocked his leg at the lid of the bin before heading south along the bridlepath, stretching his legs on a return trip to the farms of Kettleness, and the promise of a good square meal wrapped in fleece untainted by strange oils or other unpleasant Mediterranean secretions. It took him less than ten minutes to reach the borders of Harker's farm at Kettleness carried along by the scent of the seventy beef cattle corralled in the main barn. Once he was safely inside the perimeter of the farm buildings, Boldwood sought out a holding position in the shadows behind a raking machine and a thresher then began to plot his path to paradise. But he had unwittingly caught the eye of the owner of the farm, who was loading cartridges into the twin barrels of his favourite "over and under" Baikal shotgun in the darkness of his kitchen. Within very few seconds the business end of the Baikal was through the kitchen window frame and lining up on his furry contours. Then the muzzle of the first barrel boomed and Boldwood's dark hiding place became a shrapnel-filled hell. The farmer fired again, tattooing Boldwood's bloodied hide with another cloud of magnum ball bearings and metal splinters as he turned tail and fled, accidentally head-butting a bolt collar on the edge of a gate as he rushed from the farmyard to the lower fields.

★

Four fields away in the valley bottom, Dudley Kingcombe was also having an interesting evening; waking up from an unscheduled nap with a start, on the edge of his caravan bench seat just at the point at which he was about to disappear under the table, he just managed to grab a handful of curtain material in time to save himself. Once he'd managed to drag most of his bulk back from the point of no return it began to dawn on him that he had been out for the count for some considerable time. The gas fire was still on low, switched onto its lowest setting to burn off any condensation that might obscure his view of the edge of the field and the riverbank. But he sensed that something was wrong, though couldn't immediately justify his feelings of unease.

Outside it was pitch black, and no less dark inside the rolled steel walls of his new home. Then a shotgun discharged from the top of the hill in the direction of the farm. Taking care not to move too suddenly he reached over his rifle and grasped his night vision binoculars, bringing them carefully up to the bridge of his nose, looping the cord around the back of his head. Dudley braced his elbows on the Formica table top and scanned the riverbank. He could hear men shouting from the farmyard higher up and the sound of metal feed bins rolling around on the flags of the yard.

Then all the rabbits that had been playing on the riverbank suddenly disappeared. He thought he heard a soft plop on the caravan step but dismissed it. Then he heard a sound that made him freeze. It sounded almost exactly like a stag or a bull panting heavily outside the thin metal door. The heavy breathing began to fade as *the something* moved off, toward the bedroom end of his temporary home, along the concrete slab base. Dudley tip-toed to the end of the caravan in his socks, following the panting, but couldn't see anything outside below the line of the windows that might account for the noise.

Climbing carefully on the bed, he cupped his hands around his eyes and peered out through the caravan's small bedroom window; but there was nothing to see. Then the letterbox flap on the main door at the other end of the caravan swung up, so Dudley inched back off the bed and returned to the kitchen area. He could just about see that the inner letterbox plate was still extended in the gloom, so he crept closer to the door and crouched down slightly to get a better view. The stainless steel pin holding the flap squeaked again as the thin aluminium letterbox flap trembled on the top of a huge red tongue, smeared in stinking saliva. Dudley opened the fridge door, grabbed hold of a jar of Colman's mustard, discarded the lid and then shook the contents over the tongue which stopped quivering and shot backwards out of the caravan as if propelled by an elastic band. Whatever owned the tongue beyond the door went very still then launched itself into the stainless steel horse trough, beside the concrete base, panting and snarling. Several minutes passed without him hearing any other strange noises; then it seemed he was alone. Or so he thought... then "something" slammed against the caravan door.

'What the 'ell were th…' whispered Dudley, cutting himself off to listen to something that sounded like a garden rake, with several hundred kilos of malice behind it, strike the door face again; sliding down the plastic-coated steel sheet – making a noise like old fingernails being dragged across a pane of glass. Dudley tip-toed over to the table, snatched up his rifle and opened the lounge side window, pushing out the long barrel of his rifle as he brought the stock up into his shoulder. What he saw stepping down from the caravan step was something so monstrous and frightening that he almost forgot himself entirely. As the thing outside the caravan turned its rump on him and broke into a run toward the riverbank, Dudley followed the retreating beast through the Optima 10x45 telescopic sight and breathed out slowly, placing the main crosshair bar just above its front haunches, then squeezed the trigger after biting down on the huntsman's clicker between his teeth. If whatever it was had heard the pop and raised its neck to locate the source of the noise, its head would no longer have been a part of its body. But the creature ran down into a small depression at the exact same moment it cocked its ears, and Dudley's explosive bullet passed harmlessly over its head, streaking away into the darkness – until it struck the side of Albert Gall's LPG storage tank a few seconds later on the other side of Lazy Jane Lane. The bullet punched through the tank and ignited the gas, causing an explosion of such violence there were at least a dozen heart attacks and miscarriages amongst Albert's collection of racing pigeons; even though they were sheltered from the worst effects of the blast in their roosting shed at the extreme edge of his plot. Night turned to day as the lower portion of the valley was suddenly illuminated by an expanding ball of flaming Flogas that immolated his runner bean canes and fruit cages, shredded the roof of his cottage, set the canvas roof of his Land Rover ablaze and severed the electricity and phone cables to the rest of the houses and smallholdings below.

★

Down the coast, inside Mystery City, the DJ's island was now in need of some serious first aid. Although Barnett's timely intervention had put out the fire, the matt black chipboard fascia was now broken and scattered over the parquet floors after a good seeing-to from the wrecking bars and the old sledgehammer Barnett's companion, Jamesy, kept by his camping bed in the projector room.

'When ahh get ma hands on the barstard that left that focken wiring loose he'll wesh hez white focken ass was dressed 'enn chain mail.'

'Thurrs brandy stains on the bottom boards, Barn. The wee label's a bett scorched but yee can read the back. What's V-S-O-P mean?' murmured Stone, with a mystified expression.

'It's French for focken expensive.'

'There's no F on the bottle?'

'V.S.O.P – means very special old pale, ya daft c★★t!'

'Old pale? Old pale what?'

'FOR FOCK'S SAKE, JAMESY! How the fock dedd yew ever got yersell in a Technical College. It musht have been some kind o' focken miracle,' said Barnett, crossing himself as he looked up to the heavens.

'Same way yew gort yersell enn thess place... *I telt the chiefy – if I didnae get in, I'd break hez focken chenn!'* chortled Stone, grinning demonically.

★

Inside Valley View Bungalow at Kettleness another conflagration was making its mark. Albert "Albie" Gall had had just enough time to yank a napkin-sized piece of quilt to the top of his eyebrows before the greatest portion of his roof tiles were reduced to a great dust cloud filled with fast-flying shards and splinters sliced off by the pressure wave of the explosion – a split second before a gigantic sheet of flame rushed through his roof timbers. Then a dreadful silence punctuated by the soft crackle of withering flames descended over his plot. Albert cowered whimpering with fear for several minutes before he dared to look out from under his bedclothes. As the fall of debris and dust began to slow he risked opening his eyes and then moved his legs gingerly to check they were still attached to the rest of his body as he surveyed his Artex-covered bedspread. His bedside lamp was no longer working so he fumbled under his valance for his torch until he could feel the handle then dragged it up onto the bed, pointed it at the ceiling and thumbed the switch. The air was filled with fine white dust but he no longer had a ceiling or even the bare remains of a loft. The only things between his eiderdown and the stars were the smoking ribs of his roof and a few tile shards that clung stubbornly to their nails. His chimney breast had been decapitated and his home was in ruins. In his shell-shocked state, he was suddenly convinced that the United Kingdom had been targeted by nuclear weapons and World War Three had come to Kettleness.

He decided if he was going to die of radiation poisoning, he wasn't going to stay in a ruined house. Peeling back his quilts he shook the debris out of his slippers and put on his dressing gown, washed the dust off his scalp at the kitchen sink and opened the door to look at the desolate, post-nuclear landscape of the world he had once known and loved. No mushroom cloud was yet visible on the horizon, but Albert had seen enough Channel Four documentaries on the subject of nuclear conflicts to know that the site of the attack was probably RAF Staxton Wold, some twenty-five miles away. The blast had covered his plot with a grey dust which he reasoned was ash and radioactive material. There was too much of it for him to have any illusions about his fate. So he opened the fridge and grabbed the first of the last four bottles of Theakston's Old Peculier, followed by two small but very potent demi-bottles of Pebbletrees 'Owd Bob, then muddled about looking for the keys to his Land Rover, and his Wellington boot socks. He knew he only had a brief amount of time left before he was overcome by the effects of the radiation poisoning and was determined to spend his last few hours watching the sea, full of good beer, in his Land Rover, before he met his maker.

*

Meanwhile, back in Whitborough's most dangerous nightclub, another life-changing event was about to take place in the remains of the DJ's island.

'Some daft barstard's left a wee tullbox ennside the underneath cupboard,' muttered Jamesy – Barnett's comrade in arms – going down on his knees where the dance floor met the wall of the DJ's booth. 'It's a focken Snap-On!' he crowed, beaming with pleasure.

'Snap-On? They the tools cumpnay, no?' enquired Barnett, chipping in.

'Aye – top focken tools, Snap-On, Barn. Best focken spanners yee can buy. Or pench,' he cackled. 'A wee box like thess – shudd bee two hundred quedd – o' any c**t's money – an' that's focken emptay!'

'Two hundred quedd – forra focken tool chest! Weyll dinnae stand around admiring ett ya soft c**t. Open the barstard dupp!'

James Stone grabbed the sooty corners of Brian Drake's precious tool chest and dragged it towards the edge of the carpet, grunting and swearing under his breath.

'Is the c**t locked, Jamesy?'

'It's focken heavy!'

'Ahh shett!'

'Y'okay pal?'

'Aye, jusht blacked my bloody hands.'

'Meks a change from the glue, no?' smirked Barnett, as his friend swore under his breath.

James Stone let go of the tool chest and pushed back the clasp, then lifted the lid and gasped – slapping the palms of his black hands over his face as he looked through his fingers at the heap of gold and jewels crammed into the drawers and lower void of the chest.

'FOCKEN HEYLL…' muttered Barnett. 'WHAT THE FOCK!'

The two gangsters couldn't believe their eyes. Or their good fortune. In the space of thirty minutes they had moved from one kind of extreme to another; from potential disaster to a place, or possible new future, which was so new and unfamiliar that they couldn't yet absorb their good luck. All their years of plotting and struggle were suddenly meaningless

– and unimportant and insignificant – and forgotten… as a life-changing fortune lay before them in a blackened metal tool chest. After a very long pause, Jamesy got up off his knees and sat down heavily on one of the red velvet benches.

'Couple o' drams wud go down weyll the now, Barn – what d'yee say…?'

'Aye old fraynd… I'll jusht lock the wee dooers. I think we might be up a few hours yet.'

After a long pause, Barnett rubbed his chin and looked very hard at the scorched frame of the DJ's island. 'Jamesy?'

'Aye?'

'Dedd yee do anything aboot that wee gas leak enn th' keg store after the donkey, pal?'

'No' yet. There wuz hardly anything cummen oot the pipe – just a tiny wee hess on the elbow joint where ett cumms through the woll. Ahh put some more duct tape ooer the crack. I colled the freggen Gas Board twice but ahh couldnae get thru'. It's no' a problem. I left 'em a message an' dropped the twats a note.'

'Left 'em a message an' sent 'em a letter?'

'Aye – dedd ah mess sumthen?'

Barnett grunted with satisfaction then gave his friend a crafty smile.

'In a wee while, ya can go and gev that bloody joint another keck – an' thess time your're gonnae make it a gudd one. We're gonnae have ourselves another wee fire, an a begg bang. A proper begg one…'

'D'yee mean a proper arson? Focken champion!'

'Aye. Demolition arson…'

'But where are we gonnae stay – if we're burnen thess place doone?'

'We're off tae Spain, Jamesy. An' we're no' cummen back.'

'Spain! FOCK! I focken love Spain, focken paella! Focken sunshine…! FOCK… But what aboot MI5?'

'Fock 'em.'

'Fock 'em… yee cannae get away frum Sean Connery! They'll hunt ush doone an' kell the both of ush! We cannae leave the focken county – let alone the focken country…'

'We can go where we focken like – if they thenk we were stell enside here when thess place blows. They'll nae bother going through all the rubble looking for bits o' me an' bits o' yew. They'll jusht level the lot in an' put a concrete raft ooer the top. We're as good as dead already. Anyways these MI5 – they're no' like Sean Connery, Jamesy. They're jusht focken pretty boys. They'd focken shett themselves if they ever gort enn a ruck wee yew.'

'AWWW, THAT'S BRULLIANT BARN! Hey, if ahm dead – I can change ma name!'

'Aye. Ya can coll yersell whatever yee want – ya soft c★★t. Grandma focken Giles for all I care… Dedd the Guinness cum enn?'

'Aye – ten barrels. Ya did say ten, no? Ya know what, Barn, we cudd coll ourselves Ronnie and Reggie, no?'

'Are y'oote yerr focken mind?'

'No? Ye can be Ronnie?'

'You're no' calling me a poofter are yee, pal?'

'No, Barn! I wouldnae dae tha'! I meant the Krays wuz twenns, y'know?'

'Wull ye stop focken rambling like a c★★t! We're gonna bee nice an' low profile the now. We're gonnae be legit! As soon as I sort uzz oot wee new identities, shouldnae bee too deffacult.'

'Legit… ez tha' what ya coll a Scot that moves tae Spain?'

'Jamesy?'

'Aye?'

'Shut the fock up.'

'Barn?'

'Afore yee get tae kecking the gas pipe, move the Guinness barrels closer tae the gas pipe joint. In a nice wee half-circle. Guinness kegs are the next best theng tae a bomb that we've got. When the gas explodes an' those thengs pop they'll breng the whole focken back wall doone.'

'Ma Nan used tae say that Guinness was gud for yee.'

'Aye – the black stuff it is. It's the bloody gas cartridge in the keg that'll blow yer skull tae bits. But seeing as there's nowt but fresh air an' specks o' shite in yurrs yull be fine.'

'Hey – I've done okay fo' masell. Yer gonnae need me one day, so you'd better trett me right. How long have I gort tae pack?'

'We're no packen.'

'No?'

'No… Cuz we're dead. Dead men dinnae pack cases.'

'Canna take ma passbook fo' the Royal Bank?'

'Jusht go an' keck the focken gas pipe, an' leave the inside door open. Then tunn one o' the rengs on the gas cooker on. Make shure there's a pan on top. Put some soup or melk enn… actually – fell the focker upp frum the taps and bung tha steam pudding in the now. We're gonnae blow this place tae smithereens.'

'Canna take shome o' ma glue, Barn?' asked Jamesy, sheepishly.

Chapter Four

A Skirmish with Land Rovers.
And the Strange Case of the Beastie
in the Debenhams Quilt Cover.

Dudley watched the dust settle over Albert's plot in darkness from the next field and wondered whether the owner of the old bungalow was dead in bed, or just too shocked to move. The brightness of the explosion had temporarily hobbled his night vision and all he could see were residual flashes of whites, reds and yellows from the fireball of the gas tank explosion – fading into blacks and strange reddish-purple worms at the edge of his vision. He knelt down and closed his eyes for a few seconds, squinting to try and clear his sight, resting the stock of his rifle on his thigh. Then took a few deep breaths. He was a little puzzled when he heard panting on the other side of the hedge. There was also a new scent nearby of singed fur from the other side of the big gate.

Albert was now well on the way to rolling drunk as he staggered out of his front door and climbed unsteadily into his SWB Land Rover. Gulping down the last few mouthfuls of his last bottle of 'Owd Bob, before tossing the empty bottle into the black smoking stumps of his bean cane trellis, he pulled out the choke button on the Land Rover's dashboard plate and turned the ignition key after depressing the clutch –

as he always left his "Lillybet" in first gear, like most sensible countrymen, to save his handbrake. The engine shook itself into life and began to settle into a gentle throb. Then Albert became aware of a man, in a Russian fur cap and camouflage clothing with a rifle slung over his shoulder, climbing over the five bar gate on Conn Thatcher's boundary, opposite the end of his drive. Albert didn't hesitate and was soon bearing down on the Russian parachutist, who had arrived in his beloved village so soon after the destruction of his home, forcing the intruder to jump back over the gate head first before he was crushed by the Land Rover's bodywork. Oddly, instead of trying to shoot back, the Russian started to yell and shout at him in some strange dialect which didn't sound at all like any eastern European language that Albert had ever heard; though Albert wasn't going to stick around for the rest of the Warsaw Pact armies to arrive. He forced the protesting Land Rover into reverse gear and floored the accelerator again just as something resembling a huge black rug landed on the cargo net over his bonnet; it seemed to have the usual number of legs and two very queer arms, but it was very hard to tell exactly what it was in the dark through a windscreen obscured by scorch marks and heaps of ash. Albert thumbed the windscreen water-jet button to clear his vision and set off apace. Cavalier and carefree under the influence of half a bucket of Theakston's and Pebbletrees' strongest brews, Albert broke into song; careering down the hill singing the "Road to the Isles" whilst travelling as fast as his tyres and the limitations of the Land Rover's chassis could carry him. As his speed picked up and the last of the ash and dust blew away, he began to take in a few more of the details of his mysterious passenger. His first thought was the realisation

31

that he had picked up an enormous angry dog that seemed to be rabid or crazed because it had the biggest, maddest yellow eyes he had ever seen on an Alsatian. It also seemed to have trapped its tongue in the windscreen wiper hinge and was desperately trying to free itself. Albert wasn't at all sure that it didn't have hairy hands where its paws should have been, but after all the Old Peculier and 'Owd Bob he had imbibed its strange physiology didn't seem all that important.

As Dudley watched the Land Rover's jerky progress he was still trying to guess how the owner of Valley View Cottage could have found out about his part in the destruction of his home when he saw the mysterious beast of the field leap onto the bonnet of the bodywork which had very nearly crushed him. Then the old vehicle swung violently backwards in a mash of gears and revs, jerking left and right as its driver fought to keep all four wheels on the road; shooting forwards again in the same unpredictable manner it ran on into the darkness down the steep twisty mile of Lazy Jane Lane.

By the third bend on the lane Albert was no longer in control of his Land Rover or the correct order of verse. He had picked up too much momentum to safely navigate the tight downhill bends and was desperately trying to stay on the road for as long as he could, while he picked out a favourable piece of hedge to cushion the crash which was now a foregone conclusion. The thing on his bonnet was desperately trying to turn itself around in order to increase the odds of making a survivable dismount, but his tyre squealing plunge down the lane wiped out any chance of his passenger surviving their descent unharmed. The Land Rover ran on as Albert's drunken feet tried to depress the brake pedal that was now jammed high in its slot by the beer cans and feed sacks that had slid forward from under his seat. He took the corner after the Chapel at 40mph on two wheels with one eye shut then the Land Rover veered off onto the crushed stone path leading to the bungalow of his nearest neighbours, Mr and Mrs Coote. The old path was normally taken at a genteel 10mph at most – due to its less than perfect surface and the sharp left turn at the end of the track onto their plot. At the apex of the turn lay the rump of a grass verge, before a small culvert and a sharp drop onto the lawn and vegetable garden. Albert managed to shove his generously padded dog's bed in front of his chest before the Land Rover, now running at 45mph in neutral, hit the take-off point at the top of the verge. "The Bonnie, Bonnie Banks of Loch Lomond" were as far away as they had ever been, but the heavily planted sides of Mr and Mrs Coote's pond were a good second choice for a man who had a long rest in front of him before he got out of the fractures clinic.

Boldwood – Albert's temporary passenger – had lost all thought of blood and meat. His struggle to dismount the careering Land Rover had only bound him tighter to the cargo net tray and the rope lattice sack on the bonnet. He had tried to bite the flimsy windscreen wiper in his panic only to trap his tongue painfully in the hinge which meant his nose had been bouncing off the thick perspex windscreen panel all the way down the hill. Now the vehicle seemed to have left terra firma and was sailing through the darkness to an appointment with something hard. He managed to free his pinched and painful tongue just in time to meet Mrs Coote's washing. A king size floral quilt cover was the last thing Boldwood saw before the front of Albert's Defender dug into the turf and pitched forwards onto its roof before bouncing up and over again onto the tailgate, slewing over onto its left side and crashing into the pond. Stagnant green water began to glug through the smashed windows and ruined body panels, as the combatants struggled to shake off their concussions, before sinking into the pit of sludge and algae, watched by a gang of grinning gnomes in yellow dungarees. Albert managed to crawl through what was left of his door window, throw up over the moaning creature obscured by the saturated bed cover, wade to the edge of the pond and collapse in a drunken heap on the ornamental grasses.

Mr Boldwood – still the werewolf and now nursing a broken jaw, smashed pelvis, ribcage and two broken feet – had started to come around and began to feel his way through the slippery shallows of Mr and Mrs Coote's pond, wincing as his body attempted to repair itself, just as Mrs Coote arrived in her dressing gown and proceeded to beat him about the head with the sole plate of one of her husband's more substantial golf club drivers until she heard the groans of her traumatised neighbour behind her on the ornamental grass.

'Oh GOD it hurts,' groaned Albert, trying to push himself up on his elbows as his neighbour, Mrs Coote, finished bludgeoning the strange creature in her quilt cover.

'Albert Gall – you're going to pay for this. I've rung the police – and you can get your lazy backside off my ornamental grasses.'

'I'm dying… the Russians have landed.'

'YOU'VE BEEN DRINKING – HAVEN'T YOU? I can smell it on your breath.'

'WE'RE ALL GOING TO DIE. THEY'VE DROPPED THE BOMB!'

'What the hell are you talking about – you stupid old fool?'
'THE BOMB!'

'The bomb? What bomb?'

'*NUCLEAR WAR! We're all going to die, you stupid woman!*'

Well I thought I'd heard it all, living in Whitby. This is the first time I've had a senile old hooligan crash his Land Rover in my pond and blame it on Armageddon.'

'There's *Russian parachutists* on top of Lazy Jane.'

'Well she better get herself out from underneath them then – hadn't she?'

'But…'

'BUT NOTHING! And what's this great thing in my quilt cover – is this your animal?' said Mrs Coote, prodding the unconscious form of Mr Boldwood's werewolf with her golf club.

'I don't know… AHH – AHHH – HAHHHH… OW!' groaned Albert, as one of his other fractured ribs popped its mooring.

'Don't know? Don't know? It was on your Land Rover! You wake me up, demolish my garden, shred my washing, tell me it's Armageddon and Whitby's full of Russians. The only Armageddon you'll be seeing is the bill you'll be getting for all this lot! What's the matter with you?'

'I've broken my ribs… *and things…*'

'GOOD!'

'Eileen Coote – *you're a cruel woman.*'

'*AND YOU'RE A DRUNK!* Now I'm going in to change, my husband can come out and deal with you.'

'BUT I NEED AN AMBULANCE!'

'*IF WE'RE ALL GOING TO DIE, NOW WORLD WAR THREE'S STARTED – IT'LL BE A WASTE OF TIME CALLING FOR ONE, WON'T IT?*' shouted Mrs Coote as her parting riposte.

Boldwood began to come around again and started whimpering in his agony.

'Good doggy,' said Albert, to the quivering form trying to stand inside the soaking wet shroud of Egyptian cotton, 'if I was you, son – I'd make myself scarce, before that sour-faced old witch comes back with 'er 'usband. He's not exactly a ray o' sunshine either.' Then Albert passed out with a long sigh of discomfort, finally succumbing to the pain of his injuries and his six-bottle beer binge.

Boldwood's werewolf was no longer in the mood for any sort of carnage for what remained of his first night as a caravaner; even though he was still very hungry. His hide was covered in bleeding sores from Conn Thatcher's silver-oxide-coated magnum shotgun pellets, he was shivering cold from Mrs Coote's pond, he was bruised, battered, dizzy with concussion and throbbing with fractures; and there was a steel Land Rover windscreen wiper blade embedded in his tongue.

To compound his misery, his ears and tail had been scorched black from the explosion of Albert Gall's gas tank at Valley View Bungalow as he jumped the gate on Lazy Jane Lane. If he had been human someone would have pulled a sheet over his head. Luckily for Boldwood his lycanthropy meant he had almost limitless power to heal from almost anything except a decapitation. But tonight he felt he had suffered enough and began to limp away from his latest mess with as much dignity as he could, whilst still wearing the tattered remains of Mrs Coote's bedding.

★

At the home of Jackson Alger, Kettleness's community policeman, the phone began to ring.

'Damn it…' snapped Jackson resentfully, 'can't people just leave me alone in my own bloody bed for one night!' After a few seconds trying to get himself together and shake off his fatigue he made it to the hall where the telephone continued its relentless bullying alarm call. Jackson screwed up his eyes and let go of an enormous yawn before picking up the receiver.

'Hello? Hello! Jackson? Jackson! It's Mrs Godber. Jean Godber on South Heights.'

'Yes, Mrs Godber…What can I do for you?' he asked with a careful tone.

'You'd better wake yourself up, lad… A bomb just went off on the other side of the valley.'

'A bomb… do you mean there's been an explosion?' he asked, suddenly alert.

'Well you don't get one without the other.'

'Mrs Godber… has something caught fire?'

'Yes – right after it blew up. And another thing – someone's been blasting away with a shotgun on Harker Farm. Are you going to get out and investigate it or not?'

'Yes, of course, Mrs Godber. I'm just trying to get as much information as I can before I set off. Did you notice which property the explosion happened on?'

'Albert Gall's by the look of it.'

'Have you called the Fire Brigade…'

'No – *I'm calling you.* By the time that lot get themselves and their engine up there, there won't be anything left to put out.'

'Okay, well I'd better call them on my way.'

'You needn't bother…there's nothing on fire now… not anymore, just a lot of smoke. It looks to me like his roof's been blown off. You'd better called an ambulance instead.'

'Oh! Well thank you for letting me know. And you're sure you heard gunfire on Harker Farm?'

'I know what gunfire sounds like, we do live in the country. There were six shots at least from the farm. There was a rifle shot afterwards, too, right before the fire. In the lower field. Do you want me to send our Pete to meet you up there?'

'No Jean. Thank you for offering. Tell him to stay in bed. Besides… it might be dangerous.'

'Please yourself.'

'Thank you for letting me know. It's very much appreciated.'

'Well – don't say I didn't warn you. OH! I almost forgot. Albert's not there.'

'How do you know?'

'I've just watched him drive his Land Rover off down Lazy Jane Lane; he was picking up a bit o' speed. The funny thing is he's not come out the other end yet. I think he must have crashed, or stopped for a pee. He's always stopping on the lane to pee. I don't know why he thinks he can just stop and pee on the verge in front of respectable folk when he's got a perfectly good toilet at home, I think it's disgraceful. It's not as if he's got a medi…'

CLICK.

'Jackson… JACKSON?'

★

Dudley re-attached his trigger guard, slung his rifle across his back and slid swiftly over the gate. He could still just make out the fading glow from the red tail lights of Albert's departing Land Rover so he set off at a run after the vehicle, guessing it was going to come to a sudden halt within a very short space of time. Within another few seconds it was swallowed up by the darkness and lost behind a curve in the road below his sightline; but he could still hear its progress as it creaked and rumbled along, gaining extra momentum on its path to what was almost certainly going to be its final resting place. Then there was an eerie silence before Dudley heard a great dull thud and an enormous splash.

★

PC Jackson Alger climbed hurriedly into the cold, condensation-filled interior of his navy blue police Land Rover and turned up the heater and fan to the max as soon as he heard the engine fire up. Then he turned on his disco lights and selected first gear, rejecting his seat belt in favour of a packet of Rothmans. Once he could see a reasonable amount of the outside world, through the mist on his windscreen, he set off in a squeal of rubber once he had radioed the station in Whitby; he then tore across the valley to Albert's wrecked bungalow. Halfway up the other side of the valley, below Chappell Heights, he caught sight of a woman in a nightdress with a golf club on the Cootes' back lawn, standing over a tubby bear-shaped animal underneath a huge tablecloth. There also seemed to be something that looked like part of what had once been another Land Rover in the pond. But before he knew what was happening he had scooped up Dudley Kingcombe and driven off the road into the soft embrace of a very old piece of hedge; though it wasn't soft enough to prevent him cracking his nose on the steering wheel and breaking his collarbone on the metal instrument panel when the hedge bit back and seized his car's wheels in its tangled roots.

★

In the kitchen of Harker Farm the Thatcher menfolk were coming to terms with the true character of their adversary. And a draining board full of smoking shotgun shells. 'I reckon you must have winged it, Conn, there's blood spots all ovver the yard out t'cattle grid, what the hell was it?' asked Wilf Thatcher nervously, shining his torch into the dark corners of the yard at Harker Farm.

'Looked pretty much like a werewolf to me,' said Conn Thatcher to his younger brother, matter-of-factly. 'Shall we get vet'nary out for a second opinion?' he added, pulling the last spent cartridge from the smoking barrels of his Baikal shotgun.

'Conn, there's no such things as bloody werewolves, y'daft beggar.'

'Well, I reckon my eyes are alreet. But I reckon yours are gonna 'ave a big fallout with that thing between yer ears then, Wilf lad. Sometimes, you'd do well to thank yer eyeballs for letting you know how the world really is and tell yer brain to keep its gob shut.'

'But…'

'But nowt. We're gonna keep this to our sens – reet? I'm not having that bugger Albie Gall an' all that lot in valley bottom smirking cos they think we're losing our marbles. We'll keep our gobs shut. Just like Jack Farrar's done. Jack's known about these bloody things for years... Now gee us your torch, I'm going down inta Low Field to the road.'

'On your own?'

'Aye. I've put four shots in it. Time to finish it.'

'But if it really were a werewolf – how you gonna kill it wee them shells?'

'Cos I 'aven't shot it with regular shells – *these* is Thatcher magnum specials,' snapped his brother, tossing a shotgun cartridge at his next of kin.

'EH?'

'I took out the pellets to treat 'em – daft lad. Then re-crimped the heads.'

'Treat 'em? Treat 'em wee what... Mr Muscle drain cleaner?'

'Silver oxide. Melted a couple o' tablespoonfuls in a skillet then hot-dipped the pellets. Should slow the bugger down, till I can finish it off.'

'How you gonna do that?'

'Like Henry the Eighth finished off Anne Boleyn – *wee this*,' added the farmer, pulling out a polished cutlass from under the feed sack on their farmhouse kitchen table.

'Blummin' 'eck! That should do it! Is that bugger as sharp as it looks?'

'Sharp as it needs to be for what I've got in mind.'

'Where'd you find it?'

'In the priest hole a couple o' year back. Had a mind to take it to Acorn Antiques, but I haven't had time to get round to it, any road, lucky I've still got it. Might see some more action yet. Go fetch Grandfer's old Webley pistol from the

41

biscuit tin in the boot room and we'll check around the yard first an' the outbuildings. Just don't let the bloody dogs out. Once we've done that I'm going after it if I can find a trail.'

'Wharrabout that Dudley Kingcombe fella int caravan?'

'Reckon Dudley's doing his bit. But you know what they say... two guns in the hand is better than a copper in the bushes. I ain't giving anyone round 'ere the right to say I'm a bloody coward. By the way, the bullets in Grandfer's Webley are hollow point specials. So be bloody careful where ya point it – reet?'

★

Jackson's collision with Dudley and the foliage of Lazy Jane Lane had been overheard by Mrs Coote who dispatched her husband to grumble over Albert and his handiwork, whilst she revved up to new peaks of fury over the second crash opposite their access road. Armed with her golf club and a new resolve to deal out another helping of summary justice she adjusted her housecoat and set off up their drive to investigate the car horn and the flashing blue lights on Lazy Jane Lane. When she arrived at the scene of the second automobile accident of the evening it was not as a citizen who retained any residue of deference for the forces of law and order.

'*I see you've been drinking as well, Jackson Alger,*' said Mrs Coote as she bent down to the window of Constable Alger's car; its nearside buried in the hedge opposite the top of their drive on Lazy Jane Lane. 'Did you know you've got a man, with a rifle, jammed under the brackets on your roof?'

'OWWWWWW!' groaned the constable as he felt the broken bridge of his nose.

'Serves you right for not wearing your seatbelt. You should be setting an example but since you're here in a hedge with an unconscious, armed man on top of you – you can go and arrest that lunatic Albert Gall and his new dog. They've passed out on the edge of our pond – as drunk as Oliver Reed. They've ruined my lawn and our pond. And my best Debenhams quilt cover…'

'OWWWW…'

'Are you going to get out and do your job – or are you just going to sit in that police car of yours moaning all night?'

'Mrs Coote… why are you carrying a golf club?' asked Alger, still too dazed and confused to manage anything but the simplest verbal exchange, gritting his teeth as he tried to support his throbbing shoulder, whilst his nose dripped blood into his lap.

'Oh… you noticed my golf club did you? Mr Coote and I often have a game of golf – after we've chased the Land Rovers off the lawns of an evening. It helps us wind down before we go back to bed – and what do you do to wind down before bed, Jackson?' she asked, arching her brow sarcastically as she swung her club carelessly onto her shoulder. 'I keep one of these drivers beside the wardrobe too just in case someone tries to strangle me in my bed.'

Jackson couldn't think of anyone who was more able to defend herself than the woman now standing beside his door, but was too polite and in too much pain to say so.

'Mrs Coote, could you open my door for me please… I think I've broken my arm.'

'I suppose you want me to call you an ambulance as well, do you?'

Dudley, who was sprawled across the roof of Jackson's police car, now began to come around only to discover his arm was stuck fast underneath the light bar cluster on the patrol car's roof all the way up to his shoulder – and his left thumb was pointing back towards his elbow.

'And I suppose he'll want one as well, will he?' asked Mrs Coote, prodding Dudley's ribs with her golf club.

★

Thirty minutes later, in the kitchen of another farmhouse far away in rural Devon, another phone began to ring.

'Beere Farm! OOOs thess?'

'Ma?'

'Dubby! Do eee know what toime it ez? What yoube ringing uzz up for this toime o' noight?'

'Sorry 'bout the toime, Muthurr. Oi needs you ta send me zum cash in the mornen.'

'What's wrong about ringing uz enn the mornen then? You just got yerr old Ma out o' bed y'know?'

'Well oi wanted ta be sure to catch eee now, cuz oim in a bit o' bother.'

'A bit o'bother… what's that then…?'

'Well, it's a long story, but one o' moi bullets just hit some bugger's LPG tank. In the garden o' the 'ouse opposite the farm. Blew the roof off the poor bugger's bungalow.'

'*Holy smoke Dubby,* you ain't killed nobody ave eee, bay?'

'No, Ma. Nobody's dead. The only thing that's dead iz moi bleddy wallet.'

'Well, thank the Lord for that. In all the years you bin killing, this must be the first toime you've shot yourself a bungalow.'

'That aint funny, Ma…'

44

'HUH! Well neither is getting yerr old Ma out o' bed –
for your bleddy wonky eyes. Tiz a good job no-one down
yerrs gonna foind out. You'd be a bit stuck for work... Ain't
you got insurance though – from Kivells? You don't wanna
go scratchen' 'oles enn yer own pockets, bay.'

'I don't want this getting out, Ma. I wants ta keep a lid on
it. If we can find this fella in th'ospital – the one who's lost his
roof – 'fore 'ee starts blabbing – we can hush it up. An there
ain't nuthenn wrong with moi eyes, okay. Two thousand
should be enough.'

'Two thousand! What you bin using up thurr... a bleddy
naval gun! Oi can't be sending that much in the mail you
know.'

'Not the mail, Ma... Oi means get the bank to transfer ett
to the Whitby branch o' the Midland zo oi can peck it meself.'

'Oh alroight. What dedd the police say?'

'It were them that arranged it.'

'The police told eee to take pot shots at some bugger's gas
tank? Policing's a bit diff'rent up thurr then, Dud, eh? You'll
need a bit more than two grand to keep this fella's gob shut
oi reckon.'

'Ma! Oim up 'ere 'cause they says they got a begg cat
problem, an' they weren't tellin' fibs cos oi seen the bastard.
An' it ain't no bloody Panther oither. Must be the beggest
bloody runt Alsatian-cross that's ever lived. An' I ain't so sure
it weren't rabid...'

'RABID! Lord save us an' 'elp us! Don't you go taking no
risks now, Dud. What koind o' cross do eee reckon twaz, bay?'

'What do oi reckon twaz? Crossed with a bloody
wolverine an' the 'ound o' the bleddy Baskervilles, I reckon.
Nastiest looken bugger you ever saw. You've wouldn't want

45

any o' that bastard's pups – you'd wake up with no bleddy toes or fingers. Jus' moi bad luck oi missed umm. Bugger ran into a gulley just as oi took a shot. Anyways, Ma, damage is done. Can eee jus' make shure oi gets me cash. I gotta go now. Constable Alger's mates frum Whitby station is putting me up for the night until we sorts it out.'

'Sounds like yoome been 'aving a time of it, Dud?'

'The police don't seem ta loike thurr seatbelts up yerr.'

'Well you tell that fella you wuz dealing with we 'ope eees alroight.'

'Oi well, Ma.'

'Oh… one other theng. When you gets 'ome – after you killed that bleddy wolverine or whatever twaz – you can go see Ella Furnish. She's just got 'er divorce through. Take 'er zum flowers. It's about toime you got your leg over. Oi wants some bloody grandkids 'fore you get locked up… are you listnen? An' try not to ruin any more blummin' 'ouses.'

'No courting for me for a foo weeks. I broke me bloody thumb.'

'Don't need no thumbs for shagging… owd eee do that?'

'Broke it on the poliss Landy.'

'You punched a bleddy Land Rover?'

'No – the bleddy theng ran into me!'

'If I wuz you, bay, oid get meself back yerr. Sounds loike they'm all madz-hatters in Whitby. Roight – is that it for tonight? I'm too long out me bed.'

'Two thousand, Ma.'

'An' you can get your bleddy eyes tested when yoome back 'ome, bay.'

★

Conn Thatcher couldn't find any trace of his yellow-eyed adversary or his guest assassin once he had reached the edge of Lazy Jane Lane, though he certainly saw what had caused the bright orange flash just beyond the top of the valley. An act of God was probably a fitting description of the calamity that had been visited on his irksome neighbour, Albert Gall, as the top of his bungalow appeared to have been lifted off and pulverised and his plot covered with several inches of ash. There was a fresh trail of muddy tyre tracks, mixed with ash, leaving the top of Albert's plot so he decided to follow the tracks as far as they led. As he got further down the hill he saw the lights of several police cars and a small group of men with an oddly-dressed interloper. So having nothing more pressing to do he decided to find out if they had standing room for another.

Further down the coast an even bigger gathering of the emergency services was soon to occur. Then the farmer heard a snarl and a self-pitying whimper from a clump of hedge down the old footpath off the left side of the lane.

Chapter Five

The Safe Disposal of Lycanthropic Corpses.
A User's Guide.

The best way to kill a werewolf is to sever its head with one stroke and bury it by a waning moon. The heart should be taken out before the burial and burnt to ash. If the head is not removed in a single cut, or the heart is left in the body, the spirit of the wolf will not be able to rest. If any blood or bodily fluid from the living animal makes contact with another living human then that person will also develop the same condition. If they were also born when the planet Mars was in the sign of Aries, in the twelfth house of the subject's birth chart. Conn Thatcher knew exactly what to do to protect himself from any contact with Boldwood's blood and saliva after studying the Comery family records box at St Hilda's Church in Whitby. Before he left the farm he folded up a recently emptied feed sack and put it in his satchel, slipped in his chainsaw gloves and then clipped his full-face woodsman's visor to the shoulder strap. Then he added a lock knife and a pair of secateurs to the pockets in his gilet in case he needed to cut through the ribcage to get to the heart of his enemy. Then he had a double scotch for courage and set off after his prey.

Chapter Six

The Awkward Last Moments of Lindsay Boldwood, Lycanthrope and Publican Extraordinaire.

The Thatcher family had always bred men with good strong arms. It was one of the physical traits that had enabled the Thatcher farming dynasty to thrive in a challenging place like Kettleness. Many of the most successful fast bowlers in the county cricket team were Thatchers. A Thatcher had won a silver medal in the men's shot put at the 1908 Olympic Games in London and a bronze in the javelin in 1948. Very few people were willing to go up against one of their men folk in a game of fists. Now a Thatcher arm and an old Navy cutlass was about to end the story of the largest, meanest werewolf to stalk North Yorkshire's desolate moors. Lindsay Boldwood's reign in blood was about to come to an abrupt end.

Conn Thatcher had spent the best part of two afternoons polishing the cutting edge of his new-found cutlass with a wet stone and a small can of light machine oil before finishing off the newly sharp edge with emery paper until the old steel shone like polished tin; then he tested it on a raw swede, from the loose vegetable racks in their larder, only to gaze down afterward in awe, as the swede and the chopping board beneath it flew apart with his first practice swing, tumbling to the floor as the cutting edge of the cutlass blade embedded itself in his deceased parents' farmhouse table.

Since his escape from Mrs Coote and her vicious golf club driver, Boldwood had struggled to mend. The silver-oxide-coated pellets from Conn Thatcher's shotgun had stymied his usually swift supernatural regenerative powers to a crawl, and he found he could barely maintain any kind of decent pace, or find the energy to shrug off the clinging wet quilt cover which showed off his numerous stigmata like a lupine version of the Turin shroud. At the top of the field, on the other side road from Mr and Mrs Coote's driveway, his "horse's coat" appendage had become entangled in a fiendishly tight stretch of the hawthorn boundary hedge and was stuck fast. Only his great shaggy head and neck had emerged from the thorns into freedom. Boldwood had temporarily given up the struggle and was taking stock of his predicament – as well as the lingering aftertaste of a giant helping of Colman's mustard – when he noticed the size 14 Wellington boots of Conn Thatcher a few inches away from his nose in the moonlight and the glint of an old but deadly blade.

'Reckon you've had the last of my rams… you ugly bastard,' muttered the farmer as he took off his Barbour jacket and put on his lumberjack's visor and gloves. 'This is gonna hurt you a lot more than it's gonna hurt me,' continued his nemesis, taking a few practice swipes with the cutlass. Boldwood became very still and looked up at his executioner, narrowing his burning yellow eyes. In the deep black lustre of his pupils the reflection of the cutlass and the farmer's raised arm lodged in his fevered brain and he closed his eyes. Then the old blade chopped down and Boldwood's head flew from his shoulders.

Chapter Seven

Disco Inferno.

Inside Mystery City Barnett had concluded he had better set up the explosion, to effect the demolition of his own club, rather than leave the preparations to his less sophisticated partner in crime. He could at least rely on his friend to pack their new-found fortune in his Celtic Football Club tote bag. And pack one change of clothes. Once he had wedged open the door in the gable end of the building which led to the keg store he set about the elbow joint at the top of the gas inlet pipe, unwinding the duct tape applied by his friend before inflicting an exploratory tap with a small lump hammer to the crack in the flux. A loud satisfying hiss, and an overpowering stench of rotten eggs, let Barnett know there was now no turning back. Satisfied with his work, Barnett quickly arranged the rest of the Guinness kegs in front of the gas pipe in a semi-circle, before swinging his lump hammer at the fractured pipe joint one last time to create a big enough split in the metal for what he had in mind. Once inside the kitchen on the other side of the building he took out a large pressure cooker, filled it with cold water and added a steam pudding to the water for the benefit of the police forensic team, then turned on the biggest gas burner, ignited the ring and slipped a wooden wedge under the kitchen door to prop it open. By the time the escaping gas from the keg store made it from one side of the old sailcloth factory to the other there would be enough flammable vapour to blow out the walls, lift the roof and obliterate everything inside. Barnett added three mixed crates of bottled spirits, and opened a five gallon drum of white spirit below the lift motor in the cellar, to take care of whatever was left of the old wooden staircase and anything that hadn't been turned to ash, or splinters or rubble, by the four-storey gas fireball.

Chapter Eight

Snakes, Ladders and Wiretaps.

Inspector Ray Marshall's house on Leather Lane was a smart, well-kept but unremarkable 1930s semi with an original wooden garage and a neat square lawn. The house also retained its period windows, with their stained glass feature inserts in the upper portion of the frames, and its original glazed door. Marshall had never been a man who spent money on his house unless it was absolutely necessary; but when anything did require attention he had always used the best tradesmen. His home was where he had enjoyed his most inspirational moments as a detective and, since his wife's self-enforced absence, it had become a second office as well as his home. There was now a double-width desk in front of the upper bay window in place of the dressing table and vanity mirror, reference books on every aspect of criminology on the shelves inside the alcoves either side of the chimney breast, in place of his wife's musical boxes, and a line of filing cabinets, or f-cabs as they were known in the service, lined up on the dividing wall. It was to all intents and purposes his own private incident room; with a scruffy single bed pushed up against the inside wall. Since his "suspension" Inspector Marshall of Whitborough Police had added a huge white wipe board to the chimney breast which he had divided into four columns under four headings: 'DATES', 'INCIDENTS', 'LOCATIONS' and 'PEOPLE OF INTEREST'. The board also seemed to be of considerable interest to his window cleaner who hadn't noticed Marshall returning to his property as all his attention was fixed on the interior of his office bedroom. Marshall tip-toed carefully over the threshold of his drive onto the lawn as the man on the ladder continued to peer through his net curtains – oblivious to his presence. He decided to hide behind the laurel bush in the corner of his garden to see what the man up the ladder did next; it was only after he turned his head that Marshall recognised the junior MI5 agent from the first meeting at the station. Very slowly, so as not to alert the man, he made himself as small as possible and moved flush with the bush.

The man at the top of the ladder took some pictures through the window on a miniature camera then descended the ladder, taking a moment to check Marshall's drive and the pavement beyond, folded up the ladder, hoisted it onto his shoulder, picked up a toolbox and sauntered off towards an unmarked navy blue Transit van, trying to look as inconspicuous as possible. When the van and the agent had departed Marshall stood up and made his way up to his front door, then glanced back at the garden and drive before he checked to see if the plastic paperclip he had inserted in between the door and its frame was still in situ, but the clip was no longer there. He opened his door and saw it had come to rest in front of the draught excluder, bent and twisted, indicating that the door had been opened and closed again. For the next few hours, before he gave up and retired for the night, he turned his house upside down but found nothing missing or out of place. Lying in bed, his thoughts began to turn to the possibility that his house had been planted with listening devices or even covert cameras; which gave him an idea. After half a day of worry and anxiety he went to sleep with a smile on his face.

The following day was a very productive one for the Inspector. He took the train to York and visited the City Library, to use their reference room and the archive, managing to get a partial translation of the Spanish on his gold coin; he also tracked down the office of Professor Lawrence Baston Demarque, but was unable to get past reception to speak to the Professor who was apparently unavailable despite being in the building. Then he went to Maplin to buy a general purpose electrical field scanner of the type used by electricians and builders to detect cables and copper pipe behind stud walls. After two pints of Centurion Ale and a pasty in the Blue Bell pub he returned to the station and took the train back to Whitborough. He walked home to Leather Lane, inserted two batteries in his scanner and drew the bedroom curtains.

Within a very short space of time Marshall had discovered two listening devices in his bedroom office, a battery powered microphone fixed to the base plate of the clock on his mantelpiece, and a larger device fixed to the inner face of the side beam on his single bed. He also found a small camera behind the leaves of a dusty houseplant on a shelf in his hall, positioned to overlook the front door, with a trailing wire that disappeared behind the wall panelling next to the meter cupboard. Satisfied with his detective work he returned upstairs to his office and broke wind several times for the benefit of his eavesdroppers, then went to bed early, but his mind was too active; after a few hours of restless turning and staring at the ceiling he decided to get dressed and go out for a walk to St Mary's Churchyard below the Castle.

Chapter Nine

The TWOC-ing Getaway.

Barnett had never used gas as a method of mass destruction. He had always preferred Molotov cocktails, or Aberdeen mafia flame cake (a taped brick of firelighters in a rugby sock soaked in petrol, bound with baling wire to increase the burn temperature). Gas was something to be avoided as its effects were unquantifiable and often unnecessarily destructive – as well as being downright dangerous for anyone involved in setting up the explosion. But it was the only game in town if a demolition or a comprehensive obliteration of evidence was required. With a mixture of fear and elation he hurried out of Mystery City's rear fire door less than ten minutes after fracturing the gas inlet pipe in the keg store. Barnett had arranged to meet his co-conspirator, Jamesy, at the end of Rope Walk and drive off in whatever car Stone had managed to steal. This time Jamesy had done them proud. Waiting for him at the junction of Rope Walk and Arguments Lane was a black long wheelbase model Mercedes 280 saloon with leather seats and a boot the size of a coal bunker. Barnett opened the boot lid, tossed in his tote bag and a small haversack alongside the Snap-On treasure chest then jumped into the passenger seat of the well-appointed Mercedes.

'Spic and span, no?' crowed Jamesy, grinning with glee as he let off the handbrake of their luxury saloon transport.

'What's that focken smeyll?'

'I had a couple o' tinnies before we left.'

'Are yew drunk?'

'I'm no'!'

'Jamesy, you've no' been on the Special Brew?'

'I telt yee, I only had the two.'

'If ya didnae have a focken peanut forra brain yee'd have nay focken sense at all. An' what wee the car... d'yee thenk yee cud pench sumthen more conspicuous next time – like a focken Rolls Royce?'

'Do yee no' like it, Barn?' asked his friend with a puzzled expression as they drove down to Foreshore Road.

'Oh aye – except whoever owns thess wull be jumpen all ooer the poliss when they find it's been focken stolen. Yudd better pray they dinnae wake up until we're oot the county.' Barnett bent down and felt for the glove compartment door catch.

'What are you looken for, Barn?' enquired his friend.

'I'm trying tae find the papers tae proove whose car we've focken necked. Keep your focken peeps on the focken road.'

'There's a wee box o' business cards enn the door pocket.'

Barnett rummaged in the bottom of the Mercedes door tray and closed his fingers on a small card, drawing it towards his eyes and tilting it towards the light of the street lamps.

'Does the wee card say who's wheels we've necked?'

'Oh aye – you've done well wee thess time, Jamesy. We've jusht necked the personal wheels o' the best mate o' the Chief o' the Poliss. Superintendent focken Desscount.'

'Whose wheels?'

'Mister focken clubland hisself… Ted focken Knight, the focken compere for tha' Battle o' the Bands!'

'Ted Knight's bezzy mates with the poliss?'

'Jamesy… the c★★ts are focken family. As soon as we get tae the edge o'toone we're swappen cars and setting fire tae thess.'

'Ya cannae set fire tae a Merc like thess – it'd be focken sacrilege.'

'I didnae get where I am leaving focken evidence lying aroond. We set fire tae the bastard or yee can drive it off the pier…'

'Are we getting the ferry frum Hull?'

'Sence we have nae got a passport I shouldnae thenk so. I'm leaven us a false trail. We're leaving the next car in the ferry port then getting a bus tae York, a train tae Blackpool, a ferry tae the Isle o' Man, a boat tae Dublin and then we're buying our own boat tae get tee Spain.'

Chapter Ten

The Big Bang.

Since his supension Inspector Marshall had been taking lots
of short walks into Whitborough from his home to exercise
his legs, and give his mind a rest from the piles of documents,
post-it notes and statements with which he was trying
to assemble a credible theory to crack the most important
criminal case of his career. The fresh air and the change of
scene were an invaluable source of relaxation for him, and
a chance to practise the art of lateral thinking. He had never
once ventured out during the evenings, just to walk, when he
was working. But now he'd forced himself out of his usual
comfort zone, he found he was rather enjoying his time out
of doors. Marshall had just entered the side gate into the
cemetery, at St Mary's Church at the end of Long Acre, when
an enormous blast shook the ground beneath his feet, and a
rising mass of flaming bricks, timber and slates rose upon a
broiling fireball from Rope Walk two streets below.

'Holy Mother of God!' gasped Marshall, ducking behind
a large sandstone block tomb, as the first chunks of broken
masonry smashed down onto the paths and the headstones
filling the graveyard. Then a stone roof tile hit a flagstone
beside him and exploded. The old policeman decided he'd
better get himself under cover as soon as possible so he

stuffed his handkerchiefs under his trilby to protect his head, turned up his collar and raced for the side door to the church before anything bigger fell out of the sky and ruined his day.

Marshall calculated that the blast was somewhere along Rope Walk or Vexing View, below St Mary's lower perimeter wall; but any thoughts of a closer inspection would have to wait. The church's anti-vandal grilles were ringing with the impact of hundreds of small chunks of brick and doing a sterling job of protecting the old stained glass, but the gargoyles holding the guttering were having a terrible time, losing eyes, ears, fingers and Roman noses as the deluge of rocks and stone rained down over the churchyard. Marshall couldn't get the church door open, despite the fact it was unlocked, but he was reasonably well protected above the waist by the stonework of the Gothic vestibule. But like Achilles, his lower legs and ankles were still horribly vulnerable. He was about to leave the door and take his chances under one of the oak benches when the heavy metal turntables of Mystery City's DJ's island flew into the vestibule and broke both of his ankles.

Chapter Eleven

The Problem with Werewolves in Hospitality.

Far away from gold and jewels in Cloughton village, the home of Whitborough's most accident-prone lycanthrope, it had been an eventful Easter weekend at the Shirestones Hotel for Lindsay Boldwood before his departure to meet his nemesis in Kettleness. The rumours swirling around the village about the strange incidents of the last couple of weeks inside the upstairs corridors, and the shocking triple murder nearby inside Crescent Moon Kebabs, had done more to drag the residents of the village away from their hearths and out into the community than the great snowfall of 1947. Two pairs of policemen were on full time patrol in Cloughton village, but had found very little to do except listen to the many theories and opinions offered by the locals. The survivors of the gruesome attack in the takeaway had fled to West Yorkshire and could not be found.

Two reporters from the Whitborough Evening News arrived in Cloughton, but found that nobody wanted to talk to them so they had returned to the newspaper's offices, and then driven to Leeds to try and find a possible link with gang wars in the Turkish business community in West Yorkshire. Their subsequent expose was bolstered by an inquiry about the design and effectiveness of wild animal enclosures at private zoos; though this earnt the editor an ear-bashing from the telephone of Lord Warner Woollens who informed the paper's "Captain" he was consulting his lawyers regarding the inference in the article to the regime and facilities of Charlwood Zoo.

Matthew and Dale Penny's panicky call for help on Sunday night, from the Shirestones Hotel, had not been warmly received at reception in Whitborough Police Station. The boys, both well-intentioned but naive young men, were still in possession of perfectly reasonable expectations and assumptions regarding the conduct and behaviour of public servants that seldom survive any meaningful first contact with officialdom.

As gigantic domestic wolves were not yet officially catered for by the veterinary profession or the police service – or the zoo and wildlife sanctuaries regulatory authority – there was some doubt about exactly which profession(s) would come to their aid on a Sunday evening, when most respectable people were watching the *Antiques Road Show* – not bothering the Sunday shift workers of the emergency services with tall stories about crazed supernatural creatures on the rampage.

Gretton's Gunsmiths, the only other business that could possibly have helped, was also closed on the Sabbath as was most of the town. Gretton's had never stocked silver bullets or explosive-tipped ammunition of any calibre; werewolves being a rare type of prey on the North Yorkshire Moors. Had Mr Boldwood acquired the ability to morph into a giant partridge, then he would have had a hundred men falling over themselves for the chance to blast him into extinction; even on the laziest Sunday evening. As it was he had been the problem no-one wanted to sign off on.

When the police had arrived at the Shirestones for the second time in as many weeks, they had found half of the glass pane in the half-glazed door to the yard on the doormat, and the rest on the doorstep; a rather embarrassed-looking chef waiting the bar and Boldwood's other nephew, Billy, left to cope with a full crowd of guests, in a state of extreme relaxation, swaying, and no fantasists to be found. Once they had checked the hotel for any other vandalism, the police had taken their leave and returned to Whitborough.

The morning after the Bingley Beach Boys' set, once his guests had gone, Boldwood had a whole day to himself due to the unexplained absence of his younger members of staff. He had, unsuccessfully, tried to contact them at home by telephone so Boldwood set about the task of cleaning the rooms and starting the laundry so his part-time cleaner, Ethel, wasn't overwhelmed when she arrived with his chef at 11am. He was less than pleased to find the broken glass pane, and a foul-smelling stain on the carpet near the telephone table on the first landing. Mindful of his recent periods of missing time, waking up two mornings in a row inside the laundry bin with no clothes on had finally convinced him he needed a few days alone, away from the village, somewhere private, to try and reconcile his mysterious health issues. But first he decided to compose another advert for new staff for the Job Centre in Whitborough; after calling his joiner to come and make more repairs. The next day he decided to bite the bullet and call his nephew, Ben, to see if he could keep an eye on the hotel.

'Hello, Ben, it's your Uncle Lindsay.'

'Uncle Lindsay, how are you, mate?'

'Well enough, thanks, Ben. Nice to hear you're still in the land of the living.'

'What d'you mean, Lin?'

'The way you ride that Suzuki XXL, or whatever it's called – it's a miracle you're not in intensive care.'

'It's an X7. An XXL is what Meat Loaf takes in a shirt.'

'Meat Loaf?'

'Yeah – "Bat out of Hell"? You know who Meat Loaf is?'

'OH! That big yank on the jukebox.'

'Yeah, that one on *YOUR* jukebox.'

'It's not me that puts the records in, you know, it's Gallup. You must have used your nine lives up by now, lad; if I were you I'd swap that bike for another.'

'Yeah – very funny, Unc. I definitely used two up getting away from that thing *in your pub.*'

'Well, *it's* not there now. And *it* had nothing to do with me; I was getting roughed up on the high street while that thing – whatever it was – was on the rampage.'

'Yeah… glad to hear you're all right, by the way. Have they caught those divvies who jumped you yet?'

'No. The police couldn't find any witnesses,' replied Lindsay, cagily.

'So it's unsolved, is it?'

'It looks like it. Next time I go for a walk round the village I'll take my baseball bat with me.'

'You could look for 'em – I could look for 'em…'

'That's very good of you, Ben, but the reason I'm calling you is to ask a favour… I wanted to ask if you'd like to stay at the Shirestones for a few days while I'm shut. I'm taking a few days off, see,' replied Lindsay, evasively. 'You can help yourself to food. Just the stuff left in the staff fridge, mind you.'

'Look Unc, I appreciate the offer, but I don't really wanna…'

'*You'll be perfectly safe,* everything's been repaired. The pub's more secure now than it's ever bloody been. There are two new solid hardwood doors at the back, and I've had an alarm installed. There's a new set of doors on the keg slide with two long locking bolts, new doors in the cellar and the scullery, with deadlocks, and a metal shutter too.'

'Can I have a think about it…'

'I need to know soon. By tomorrow night at the latest. What do you say?'

'Can I help meself to beer?'

'Well – you can as long as you can pay for it… You won't be able to use the bar pumps. I'm cleaning the lines before I go and turning off the taps. You'll have to make do with the bottled stuff if you want a drink. And don't think I don't know how much is left.'

'Right…'

'We'll talk about what you can drink if you agree to stay, and it's okay with your mother.'

'So where are you going, Unc?'

'I'm taking a few days off. I just need to get away from it all – that's all.'

'Oh… right.'

'By the way, I won't be far away. I'm not disappearing completely. I'm expecting the Job Centre to call about some new staff, so there's a chance I might have to come back briefly to interview someone.'

'You've got some new staff, Unc? After all these years?'

'No-one sticks around forever in little villages, Ben. Especially people your age,' replied Lindsay, dejectedly.

'I guess… Where are you going?'

'If I told everyone that it wouldn't be much of a break,

would it. And, by the way, this isn't an invitation to have your mates over as well. Just you – understood?'

'Absolutely, Unc… when are you going actually?'

'This Thursday night. Think you can handle it?'

'Well… you say the back door and the bogs are fixed?'

'They're called toilets, Ben. A bog is an upland swamp full of sinkholes filled with…'

'Shit… I know. Can you leave me your shotgun out… just in case that friggin' wolf comes back?'

'No. Certainly not. You can rest assured it's not coming back. If anything escapes from the zoo again you can ring them. I'm not having you blasting holes in expensive animals when I'm not insured for it. The gamekeepers at the zoo have got their own rifles. All you have to do is lock yourself in and call the reception desk at Charlwood. You'll be fine.'

'What about me bike? Can I leave it in the outbuilding?'

'Yes… But make sure it's against the back wall. If the brewery comes for my empties they won't want to have to worry about working around your motorbike.'

'If I can stay in the bridal suite and play the pool table for free, I'll do it. As long as Graham can stay too.'

'Where's he going to sleep?' asked Lindsay, suspiciously.

'Gray can doss down on the benches in the pool room, Unc. He ain't fussy, he'll sleep on a plank. Billy's not coming in for owt, is he, while you're away?'

'Billy's just going to come over to do his usual jobs,' said Lindsay, 'on the Friday after I leave and on the Saturday and Sunday mornings; he's not going to be looking over your shoulder or spying on you for me, Ben. Just remember to be nice to him. He is your cousin.'

'I s'pose I can put up with him. But he never speaks when I say hello or ask him summat.'

'He's just shy, that's all – he's just not used to talking to people generally. It's his mother's fault; she never gives him a chance to speak, and when he starts to talk she interrupts him and he just gives up. He likes you, you know. Did you know that?'

'No. I didn't. I thought he didn't like me.'

'Well – there you go then. Just nod and say hello when you see him, like you normally do. You don't have to say that much to each other.'

Chapter Twelve

The Changeling.

After having his thumb strapped and braced, Dudley Kingcombe walked carefully out of the accident and emergency department at Whitby Hospital and went into the town to buy some fruit and chocolate – and a card for the man whose house he had wrecked the night before. Once he had had a well deserved late breakfast in the Waterfront Cafe by the swing bridge, he visited the Whitby branch of the Midland Bank to collect a large envelope of high denomination notes. He then returned to the hospital ward where Albert Gall and Jackson Alger were asleep in opposite beds, dead to the world after another batch of painkillers and two heavy bowls of treacle pudding.

Dudley was still not fully mobile himself; still stiff and awkward with the bruises and knocks that only a carelessly driven police car can inflict when driven with enough momentum. He took a chair beside Albert's bed and slowly extended his sore throbbing legs, supporting his weight on his elbows until he was reasonably comfortable. Seeing Albert was still firmly in the land of nod, Dudley composed a note of apology on the back of one of the patient menus, added it to the envelope full of money and put it, with the greeting card he had bought, in the little cupboard next to his bed. Dudley closed his eyes for a few minutes, then opened them again and began to study Albert's resting form. Eventually Dudley's interest fell on the top of Albert's left ear, which was half hidden under an untidy sweep of white hair. There was something very unnatural about the shape of the top of his ear. Gripped by a sudden urge to investigate his victim's physiology, whilst nobody was looking, Dudley checked the ward was still free of staff then turned his attention back to the side of Albert's head and parted the hair around his ear. There was no doubt about it – the old man had pointed ears. What was even more peculiar was the feel of a soft downy fur covering the skin behind the lobe. Dudley was just at the point of drawing back his fingers when Albert suddenly turned his head towards Dudley, opened his burning yellow eyes and growled.

'That Mr Kingcombe's in an awful hurry,' observed the Matron overseeing Albert and Jackson's ward as she saw Dudley jump the queue on the taxi rank below the staff room at the hospital. 'He'll get himself a reputation if he starts rubbing the locals up the wrong way like that… stealing someone else's taxi right under their nose! What's he doing up here in Whitby, Sister?'

'He's staying out at Harker Farm in Kettleness for something.'

'Well he looks like trouble to me.'

'Dislocated thumb, wasn't it?'

'And bruising.'

'He's got a pair of legs like a set of fireside tongs,' she added, smirking.

'He's quite a specimen, isn't he? I hope his kids haven't got his legs, or they won't have a minute's peace when they get to school.'

'Kids! You must be joking.'

'How do you know?'

'Come on, Matron! I love John Wayne as much as the next girl, but would you want him on top of you? And John Wayne's got quite a bit more in the looks department.'

'You're *RUDE,* Deborah Mills!'

'I'm right though, ain't I?'

'It's a good job our poor patients can't hear you venting, or see your chocolate teeth, *Nurse* Mills,' added her superior, glancing at the empty box of staff Jaffa Cakes.

Chapter Thirteen

The Fugitives.

Barnett managed to contain his paranoia, in the luxurious comfort of Ted Knight's Mercedes 280, as far as the Whitborough to Filey railway crossing; before his sense of self-preservation re-asserted itself. Instructing his partner to take a fork off the main road onto a secluded wooded lane, past a small caravan site, he then directed Stone to a park up in a picnic area, screened by trees, beside a large lake.

'Right, that's far enough in this focken car. Time tae switch.'

'Awww, Barn, we're hardly ten miles away.'

'Aye, ten focken miles too far in thess. If you had a focken sign on yer head saying car thief, yee couldnae do better. We're swappen cars.'

'Wee cannae torch thess. It's a brand new Mercedes Benz!'

'It's proof we're stell walken an' breathen… You're no' gonnae cry on yer brichts like a wean, are ye'? Yew pecked the focken theng. Hand us yer cigarette lighter. There's a Ford Fiesta about a quarter mile back there. Etts a bit less focken conspicuous than this. Get the gear out…'

'Hey, Barn! Look – there's swans an' ducks!'

'Aye, very pretty… let's move, Jamesy,' muttered his boss as he watched the blue lights of two fire engines hurtling towards Whitborough a quarter of a mile away. 'Time tae make ourselves scarce…'

Chapter Fourteen

The Witch King's Legacy.

Nobody had ever been burnt as a witch in Whitborough on
Sea – or any of its adjoining parishes – since the beginning of
the reign of King Richard III. Richard, the last Plantagenet
King of England and the last English monarch from the House
of York, was also a fervent Whitborian, whose benevolent
and generous acts in favour of the town included the issue of
several Royal decrees, the first of which forbade the burning
of anyone convicted of witchcraft in Whitborough and its
surrounding districts.

Richard's edict was generally welcomed throughout the
county as it bedded into the consciousness of his subjects
and soon came to be regarded as a shrewd and merciful
act. Though, ultimately, the decree had less to do with
spreading mercy than exacting revenge upon the office of the
Archbishop of York for his sudden and excessive pursuit of
heretics, for the traditional holy bonfire, in the first months
of the new King's reign.

When the witch-finders' purge inevitably ran out of
witches, the Church unleashed its pet sadists on the poor,
the crippled and anyone born on the unlucky side of comely;
and it was not very long before there was an uprising and an
outbreak of bloody vengeance that the King was compelled

to suppress. Furious with his bishops, the king exacted his revenge by forbidding the Church from immolating any more of his subjects east of Aveyou Nympton; garlanding his decree with a threat to roll out the new edict through the whole of the Diocese of York should the Church displease him further in matters of *supplicio purgans* (purging and punishment), and reminding the Archbishop who held ultimate power in the county; so they could all get back to the business of killing the French and the Spanish instead of each other. Though there was still no absolute mercy for anyone unlucky enough to be occupying the defendant's box at a successful witch trial.

Instead of the traditional burning, the Crown's new punishment for witchcraft and necromancy in Whitborough now took the form of a trial by air and water. As a spectator event it drew crowds larger than any other method of execution in the land, and also had the useful side effect of increasing the productivity of each citizen as the execution was now invariably swiftly concluded. The new punishment began and ended with a brief confinement in the gritty bucket of Mrs Mothersole's Flying Machine – Whitborough Castle garrison's siege-breaking trebuchet – which now dispatched those marked for death, from the mortal world into the spiritual, at a height and velocity unmatched until the invention of the first ejector seat in the jet age.

It was this small adjustment of mercy that ultimately made Whitborough a magnet for witches from across the land, and a very good place for witching, especially for those who preferred to go into the next world as pioneers in the history of flight rather than as a human Roman candle. There were at least two women who freely confessed to necromancy just to fulfil their lifelong dream of flying gracefully over the sea, like the birds they so admired, before they succumbed to "Herring Flu". One succeeded in making a brief coupling with a seagull as she completed her arc over the cliffs, but her own momentum quickly curtailed their love match and she was soon brought back down to earth, pedalling furiously against the force of gravity before her final plunge into the cold depths of the North Sea.

Fortunately, most witches that arrived in Whitborough after the decree were happy to settle quietly into their own monk-like existences with the same care they had maintained outside the district's boundary.

So began a great silent emigration of occultists, wizards and witches from all corners of the kingdom to the North Yorkshire coast. From the Fens of Norfolk came the shape-shifting Penroses – into lodgings at Paradise House; the necromancing Vortenkrantzes from Ealing Common arrived to farm Peaholm Gap to the cliffs at Scalby Mills Inn fields. Mrs Mothersole's surviving relatives, and her furry familiars, rented Bloc Cottage Terrace in Cayton; and the Lawless family left Essex for Carr Marsh Farm in Aveyou Nympton where they dug busily for mandrakes, lent out wart-busting toads, and conjured the spirits of the dead with barely a murmur or a grumble from their terrified neighbours.

As word spread to the lands of the far north, another influx began. And soon the Scots began to arrive. From Dunoon came the curse-casting Bacons; from "Auld Reekie" came the faith-healing Sweeneys; by sea, came the blond Viking Thomsens from Berwick, with their old Norse gods of blood, sweat and lager; and the legendary Taggarts, with scrying mirror bowls polished with Morar sand, and pillar candles from the great abbeys of Scotland – and from Lancashire came just about everyone who had a horse or a decent pair of boots.

In Whitborough itself, several taverns adopted new names to reflect the new King's munificence. The Golden Bough became the Flying Crone, the Flower Inn became the Lady and the Gulls, and the Poorgrass Inn became the Arc of Icarus. Astrologers and Kabbalists, encouraged by the influx, filled out the weekly markets, and even Druids returned to Landkey Island to try and convince fit, strong men that building massive stone circles was the most fun they could have with a piece of string and a plumb bob. By the early days of the reign of Henry VIII, it was said that a coin tossed into the crowd on market day in Whitborough would hit at least two witches before it bounced into the sucking sludge.

Come the spring of 1983, there were no dangers left for anyone in Whitborough whose appearance or habits might have afforded them an aerial view of the headland a few hundred years before. In the Age of Aquarius, alternative lifestyles, astrology, divination and all things occult were openly discussed and practised in a way not seen since the heyday of the Vikings. The newspapers were full of astrology – rock music and popular culture were saturated with magical symbolism, art and imagery – and everybody had at least one book with a magical dragon in it. Suddenly, witches and wizards were so admired they were compelled to keep their hazel wands up their sleeves, lest they be swamped by admirers and suitors by the dozen.

Whitborough's most accomplished and secretive contemporary occultist – Sveta Anchabadze, the Sorceress of Landkey Island – was at least able to keep her admirers at bay behind the walls of Weareburgh, her castellated stone house, when the causeway to the island was accessible at low tide. The members of Whitborough's own Black Hand Coven – a band of dysfunctional minor occultists and chancers, whose exploits had much more in common with the antics of Laurel and Hardy than the rituals of the Golden Dawn – were not quite so well situated; though they were at least still unknown to the world.

Their group – formerly known by the rather less racy title of the Whitborough and District Isodora Duncan Free Dance Society – were currently lying low after the catastrophic end of their last Sabbat; which had left them one demon short, but several million pounds in the black. Though the main beneficiary of this piece of good fortune had no intention of sharing it, and had yet to convert his recently acquired wealth to hard cash. For Derek Beautimann, the Black Hand Coven had now served its purpose – and was ready to be dissolved.

The situation was further complicated by the fact that the cursed treasure was now split into three separate caches. The largest was now fermenting its own special kind of evil beneath the nylon zips of an Adidas tote bag, in the bottom drawer of a filing cabinet, in the Beautimann household's upstairs study. It was, at least, the most secure. The other half was split between two red Snap-On metal tool chests. One had been dumped behind the feeding bins of a hormonal African Black Rhino at Charlwood Zoo by its new owners, the Drake brothers. The other had been incubating under the DJ's island in a rock club run by a psychopathic Scottish gangster, but was now beginning a new chapter of its own on a very unusual route to the Irish Sea. There were also two single coins in the possession of Lord William Henry Warner

Woollens, the owner of Charlwood Zoo, and Inspector Ray Marshall of Whitborough Police; both of whom were still ignorant of the whereabouts of the recovery of the treasure, but were now on their own separate paths of discovery.

Chapter Fifteen

Watching the Detectives.

Since hobbling upstairs after his return from hospital with his feet in plaster, Inspector Marshall had been doing an awful lot of reading in the high-backed armchair he kept behind the nets of his first-floor bedroom window; only descending the stairs, on his crutches, to make basic meals and collect his post.

It wasn't until the third day that he started to become suspicious of the motorhome parked on the opposite side of the road. Leather Lane was not the kind of place that anyone with an exploring spirit and the money to afford a mobile home would choose to park for more than an hour at most. The blinds were always drawn on the side facing his house. There was evidently someone inside because he could always see lights, after dark, around the edge of its windows. But what really got his attention was the fact that, for the last two nights, two people arrived on its blindside at ten o'clock and entered the motorhome. Then 10–15 minutes later two people left. But the biggest indication that something didn't add up was the fact that both sets of people were wearing formal shirts and suits. It was either a Jehovah's Witnesses' van share or a surveillance operation team, and so far Marshall hadn't seen any bibles.

Chapter Sixteen

All Creatures Great and Small and Smelly.

Since escaping from the open window of the examination room at Bell End Vets in Aveyou Nympton, Maureen Moment's randy Parson's Terrier, Bert, had been having the time of his life. Mr Reynard's latex-encased index finger had not been the best sausage he had ever tasted, but not being particularly fussy with his cuisine he had made the best of it. The fleshy underside of the vet's fingernail had been surprisingly pleasant; once the latex examination glove came apart. His new home, a cardboard-filled soil pipe in McKenzie Dye Builder's Merchants' yard at Aveyou Nympton, was paradise compared to the rather dull and sterile environment beloved of his adopted mama which stank of mango Shake 'n' Vac, Tramp (a woman's fragrance popularised by Lenthéric), and scented candles. For a dog like Bert, home was a sensory hell on earth. Even dragging his pungent scent glands over his mother's rugs and carpets did nothing to improve matters as every delicious natural smell he brought home, for the benefit of his ungrateful mother, was obliterated under a hailstorm of air freshener spray or vindictive squirts of Dettol sanitizer.

Here in the natural world he was free to breathe fresh air and roll in as much or as little of its rich menu of odours as he pleased. His particular favourite was a good thick stripe of fox poo between his shoulders, if there were no corpses "mature" enough to rub his fur against. A decomposing pheasant on the border of his "snug" (a hay barn) was blowing up nicely, but was still a few days away from turning closer to the pleasing side of rancid.

Bert's new range also crossed paths with another four-legged creature's scent. Powerful yet fleeting. Always in the background at night. Untraceable during the day. It was the most exciting dog-like aroma he had ever come across; with definite hints of the recently deceased, round-bodied, white fluffy things, so plentiful in the countryside, that were such fun to chase.

Bert had followed the mysterious pheromone trail as far as the Three Jolly Morris Men in Burniston Village, and was resting near the pub's food scrap dustbins before continuing his hunt toward Cloughton, when he was spotted by two young men from BADCOW, the Burniston-based anarchist collective, who were in the midst of a toilet break during their regular liquid lunch.

'Hey Stigg! There's a dog 'ere, behind the barrels. It looks like a stray…'

'A dog? What's its name?'

'How the frigg would I know?'

'All right! Don't bite my 'ead off. Hasn't it got a tag?'

'Can't see one… blimey – it dunt 'alf stink!'

'What kind of dog is it?'

'It's small – and it stinks,' he replied, sarcastically.

'Yeah… what *colour is* it – you berk?'

'It's dirty white… and biscuit coloured… white mostly… scruffy looking little bugger. Kinda cute though. Have you finished in there yet?' asked Gary, talking to his buddy through the window in the gents'.

'Me zip's stuck – hang on.'

'Pull your shirt down over it and get ovver 'ere.'

'All right Gaz, 'ang on… I'm coming.' Joseph "Stigg" Barnes, the BADCOW commune's most ponderous intellectual and default jester, emerged from the rear fire door of the gents' to join his drinking buddy, Gary "Gaz" Flinton, in the car park at the back of the pub and examine the mysterious stray. Both young men taking turns to peep over the barrels at the dog resting on the pile of keg cushions.

'It's a Parson's Terrier,' said Stigg, confidently.

'Parson's what?'

'Terrier.'

'Parson's Terrier. Is that like a breed then? Like a pedigree?'

'Aye. They're like long-legged Jack Russells.'

'D'you think it'll bite?'

'Well it's not growling at us, that's a good sign.'

'Is it?'

'Yeah, usually.'

'Usually?'

'Mostly.'

'There's something stuck in its fur. Between its shoulders.'

'That's fox shit.'

'FOX SHIT! EURGH! *How did it get fox shit on its shoulders?'*

'It probably rolled in it, Gaz. Most dogs do – if they get the chance. Can you go to the bar and get us a packet of pork scratchings, and I'll see if I can tempt it out.'

'Pork scratchings?'

81

'Aye. If they don't bring 'im out, nowt will.'

'All right Stigg – if you say so. I'll ask 'em if it's theirs while I'm in there.'

Bert looked up and tilted his head appealingly at the two strange creatures, with their red and blonde mohicans, in case they had treats or dog biscuits; Bert was constantly perplexed by humans. They were never satisfied with the hair they were born with. Gary returned a few minutes later with a bag of pork scratchings and some dry-roasted peanuts.

'Peanuts?' said Stigg, puzzled.

'Yeah... they're for me.'

'Oh.'

'He looks friendly enough, dunt he,' observed Gary, 'pity we've already got one bitch... we don't need another one,' he continued, imagining Mary trying to open a can of dog food.

'It's not a bitch, Gaz – it's got balls.'

'Balls... where?'

'Behind its ears, you stupid sod!'

'I couldn't see 'em because of the crate.'

'Okay, I'll let you off.'

'Gee thanks, Stigg,' griped Gary.

'I think we should take 'im back with us; he looks like he could do with a bath and a feed... Till we figure out who he belongs to...'

'D'you think the others'll mind?'

'Nah – every commune's got a dog or a cat. And it'll piss Mary off.'

'Stigg, I do worry about you sometimes, mate – but then you do something genius! Let's get him back and clean him up. What are we gonna wash 'im with?'

'Mild shampoo and warm water should do it.'

'Head & Shoulders?'

'Nah… summat like Johnson's Baby Shampoo. I think Cass has got some, she won't mind if we borrow a squirt.'

A couple of hours later, after two baths, a shower and a blow dry in the BADCOW hut bathroom, Bert was the cleanest he'd been since he'd been born. With a mixture of pride and glee Gary and Stigg marched him into the communal lounge on a string lead for his first inspection by the rest of their gang.

'WHAT'S THAT?'

'It's a Parson's Terrier, Mary.'

'I know what a dog is, *Gary*. What's it doing here?'

'Me and Stigg thought we could use a mascot. Be nice to have an animal about the place, we're all for animals aren't we?' said Gaz.

'You can't just bring things here without asking the rest of us first. We'll have to have a vote on it. If you lose you'll have to take it back,' muttered their Fuhrer.

'Oh *chill out,* Shipley,' snapped Cassandra. 'Stray dogs are stray dogs, they don't come by appointment.'

'I wasn't…' protested Mary.

'WASN'T WHAT?'

'We can't take 'im back, he's a stray, Mary,' replied Stigg, appealing for sympathetic voices.

'The Dog Warden, then.'

'Mary – they put stray dogs down, so we can't give the poor little bugger to the warden,' explained Penny – with a hint of irritation.

'Well, where's he come from?'

'He was asleep in the yard at the back of the pub behind some kegs. Kipping on some keg cushions.'

'Take it back to the pub, then.'

'But he doesn't *belong to the pub.* That's why we brought 'im here.'

'Well what about the RSPCA?'

'What's wrong with us keeping 'im?'

'We don't have time. We're activists. We're social justice warriors. We haven't got time to be worried about…

'Animals?'

'Pets.'

'But you kidnap donkeys.'

'That's different.'

'How's it different?'

'They were oppressed.'

'How were they oppressed?'

'Because they were captives. They had no freedom.'

'They're fed, exercised and doted on. They've got their own field, they get taken to the beach every day and they've got free grub and a heated stable. You do talk a lot of bollocks sometimes, Mary.'

'WHAT!'

'Aren't you listening, Shipley? We're keeping the bloody dog; if you don't like it you can piss off. And if you aren't nice to 'im me and Stigg are gonna tell that big scary cow who owns the donkeys what you did with her asses… all right?'

'Bbbbbbut…'

'He's staying.'

'Well he's your dog and you can look after him. And don't let him on my bed. And make sure he doesn't wee anywhere,' she griped. 'And you can afford the vet's bills, can you?'

'Well, if he gets ill, your dad can pay. He's loaded, ain't he?'

'Let's have a show of hands, everybody...' suggested Penny, mischievously. 'All those in favour of keeping the dog?'

Mary turned on her heels and stormed out of the hut; mortally offended and extremely angry that she had once again been outmanoeuvred and humiliated by her peers in the commune. She decided she'd had enough of being teased and mocked and took out her Bay City Rollers purse to see if she had enough change for the bus to Whitborough. Luckily, she had enough to pay the fare without breaking into the last twenty pound note. So she crossed the road and walked towards the bus shelter.

'Well, that went well, Gaz,' grinned Penny.

'It were Joe's idea, Penn.'

'Well done, Stigg!'

'Cheers Penn. We didn't just bring him back to piss Shipsulk off. I think he's quite cute, don't you?' said Stigg, giving Bert a rub between his ears.

'Awww – look, he's rolling on his back. Has he had anything to eat?'

'He's had a packet of pork scratchings...'

'EURGH!'

'What are you going to call him, Stigg?' asked Dodger.

'What about Bob?'

'BOB?'

'Yeah, after Bob Marley.'

'What about Bilbo – after Bilbo Baggins?'

'Bilbo... that could be cool.'

'Or Rhubarb?'

'Let's write down some names and put 'em in a hat.'

'Who's got a hat?'

'A saucepan then…'

'You'll have a job, they're all in the sink.'

'Boys – you seriously need to do the washing up,' snapped Cassandra.

Chapter Seventeen

Down, Down, Deeper 'n' Down.

"Big Val" Metcalfe was one of the fairer sex's greatest natural intimidators. She was high, she was wide and she would only ever be described in polite terms as "big-boned, plush and plain". Val's favourite pastimes were donkeys, darts and "door work", though "door work" had nothing whatsoever to do with joinery, or any kind of woodwork, except perhaps to test the ability of engineered hardwoods to resist the "bounce" of the human body. Val was Whitborough's legendary freelance, self-employed door security "person". Val loved Rod Stewart, The Quo, Springsteen, doner kebabs and pizza; and didn't take garlic bread or any nonsense from anyone.

Since coming out from behind the bar of the Fleur de Lys in Whitborough to break up a gang fight, she had thumped, crushed and battered her way into the hearts of the publicans, nightclub owners and her equally frightening male colleagues in much the same way as Big Daddy and Giant Haystacks had electrified the wrestling audiences of the late 1970s. By the end of her first year working on the doors she had given up her position as head doorperson for Manshipp's Estates, who also "employed" Barnett, and was hiring out her services, as and when required, to any publican or nightclub experiencing an unsatisfactorily high level of trouble. *"One night of Val"* was enough to completely subdue any hooligan elements and keep the peace for weeks afterward. Her "fee" was always paid in cash, usually with a grateful bonus, and gave her the opportunity to spend the greatest part of her day walking Victoria Bay with her cherished herd of donkeys. Val had no need of a gym because she hauled children on and off the backs of her donkeys for four days a week and as a side effect developed deltoids and biceps as large as melons. When they had all had enough of the beach she finished off her exertions pulling their saddle-and-feed-bins cart home up the steep gradient to Ramsgill High Street and onto Queen Mary's Road.

Val was incandescent with rage when she found out that half of her donkey family was missing, presumed stolen, from their stables on the slope of Oliver's Mount. Though within minutes she was receiving more phone calls to tell her some of her missing animals had already been found, and by lunchtime on Monday they had all been recovered unharmed. But Val was not the type of lady who ever let an insult or a slight go unpunished. Whoever had stolen her precious friends was going to pay, and pay dearly, for their trouble.

When she discovered the identity of the kidnappers, from watching the tape from the hidden video camera set-up which supplemented the deliberately more prominent system already installed, she didn't tell the police. The law could do nothing that Val couldn't do better for herself; and would probably make worse. Val was a great believer in natural justice of the direct kind, delivered in person, in the first person, without the useless bureaucracy and glacial slowness of the criminal justice system. Val's system was also far superior to the courts. With a zero rate of re-offending. No-one who had ever crossed Val once ever bothered her again.

Val began her preparations for the kidnap of Mary Shipley Brown and Ian Crouch by packing her holdall with a pickaxe and shovel; then adding a roll of duct tape, wiring pincers and two insulated body bags to her abduction kit. Then she rang Terry Old, a DJ and promoter on the rock scene. Through her contact Val discovered the home of the thieves, and took a double-decker bus to Cloughton to see Burniston from upon high and locate the home of her quarry. The BADCOW scout hut revealed itself on her return journey, behind a thick hedge, in a field next to the Village Hall. Though, irritatingly for Val, the view from the top of the bus only showed the front elevation and main doors and not the side windows. But she had the advantage of a Ford Transit crew van, with black-tinted windows, in which she could conceal herself until there was an opportunity to snatch one of the thieves to administer her own brand of justice – a 48-hour vertical burial in handcuffs in Dalby Forest. She decided to wait another day or two to lull the kidnappers into a false sense of security and give herself time to find a suitably isolated spot in the woods to dig a deep enough pit. Val usually gave her victims a couple of days' grace in the forest, returning to the woods to dig them up before dumping them on the main road, without their trousers, to take their chances with the traffic.

Mary never saw Val, or registered the Pebbletrees Brewery van on Burniston Garage forecourt, as she stepped off her bus, after spending the afternoon in the Headbangers

Arms in Whitborough drowning her sorrows. Before the bus was halfway out of the lay-by Val had stepped forwards, out of the shadows at the back of the dark shiplap-clad wooden bus shelter, and swung a doubled-up rugby sock, packed with gravel, at the back of Mary's head – then dragged her into the shadows and bound her wrists with a cable tie; before applying a generous piece of duct tape to her mouth, pulling a coal sack over her head, and adding a second under her feet to cover her lower limbs.

After checking the road outside was clear Val brought the brewery van into the lay-by, opened the kerbside sliding door and dumped Mary onto a mat of large flattened cardboard boxes. In twenty minutes she was back in Whitborough ready to collect her second victim, Ian Crouch, from his shared house on Leather Lane. As Ian was nearly 6 feet 5 inches tall, even without an erect mohican, Val decided to use a different tactic to get him within felling distance at the back of the van; the decades-old evergreen "crate of beer prize" ruse which never failed. Val rung the door bell and slipped on a branded Pebbletrees Brewery cap, turning her back on the door as she checked the street for witnesses. Finally she heard footsteps on the staircase inside the front door and a key being turned in the sash lock.

'Afternoon, sir.'

'Afternoon…'

'I've come to deliver a prize for a Mr Crouch. Mr Ian Crouch?'

'A prize? What is it?'

'Are you Mr Crouch, sir?'

'Yeah, I don't remember entering a competition though. What've I won?'

'You've won two crates of Pebbletrees Black Cat lager, Mr Crouch. I just need a signature, sir, and then you can take them.'

'Two crates! *ACE!* Where d'you want me to sign, fella?'

'Just in the box next to the cross, sir,' said Val, handing Ian a vinyl-covered clipboard with an old delivery note sheet from the Fleur de Lys.

'Sorry,' said Ian, sheepishly, suddenly seeing Val's ample bosom through the front of her leather coat. 'I thought you was a bloke.'

'That's all right, sir. A lot of people make the same mistake,' replied Val, under her breath. 'Only once.'

'Say what?'

'And sign and date the chit underneath, sir,' said Val, peeling back the top sheet to reveal a blank customer address tear-off slip from her extensive collection of Boots photo-lab envelopes.

'On this slip of paper?'

'Yes, sir.'

'How many bottles did I win?'

'Fifty, sir.'

'Fifty bottles!'

'Yes, sir.'

'ACE! D'you know what... I still don't remember doing a competition. Still, mustn't grumble, eh? Bit of a result!'

'It's the one that the brewery runs every month, sir; we put the entry forms in most of the local pubs. I expect you filled one in while you were having a drink and then forgot about it.'

'Heh hey, well, I'll have to do it again some time! I can carry the other one in if you like, luv. Ain't everyday you win fifty bottles of lager, is it?' grinned Ian, rubbing his hands with glee.

'That's very kind of you, sir. They're right at the back in the van here, just behind the doors.'

Val and Ian descended the front steps of his shared house and walked towards her van which was parked in the shade on the tree-ringed forecourt. Val opened the van's rear doors and Ian bent forwards, squinting, trying to catch a glimpse of his prize.

'Sorry about the broken bulkhead light, Mr Crouch, the bulb went this afternoon,' said Val, as the gravel-packed rugby sock came out.

'What's that in those sacks?' asked Ian, with a slight tremble in his voice. Ian started to turn his head but all he could see was something that looked like a thick lumpy sausage accelerating toward the side of his face – and then his world went black.

There were many places offering solitude, peace and isolation in North Yorkshire. Val Metcalfe knew all the best, still accessible by jeep or Land Rover, from her youth. It was a long time since she had crossed the wild places she had known so well with any regularity since attaining her Gold Duke of Edinburgh's Award with the Girl Guides. But her hard-won knowledge of the North Yorkshire Moors and its most secret places was to prove extremely useful in her middle years. Especially the wild woods of Harwood Dale where Val buried Mary and Ian – back to back, up to their chins – in insulated body bags stolen from the morgue; so the cold earth and composting foliage around their bodies wouldn't kill them. Then she fashioned a crude lean-to frame over their heads from branches, and fastened them together with plastic-coated wire using her teeth and her cutting pliers, topping it off with moss and ferns. When she was satisfied that they were reasonably well protected and camouflaged she bent down and ripped the duct tape strip off her victims' mouths.

'Here's how this works. I talk first – you keep yer gobs shut,' said Val, drawing a large black machete from a scabbard strapped to her ankle. 'Any interruption, I'll tape yer cakeholes shut again, right? If you understand – *boys an' girls* – nod yer 'eads.' The two terrified punks immediately complied.

'I'm gonna be going home soon,' said Val, revealing a chipped gold incisor as she smiled. 'Nice big plate of fish 'n' chips, an' a few beers. I might even watch a film. If I'm in a good mood after all that, I'll come back and dig you up in a couple of nights – before you expire. But if you was to tell anyone you were out 'ere, when you get yer freedom back, or tell anyone else how unkind I've been you'll be coming back 'ere for good. If you understand – *boys an' girls* – nod yer 'eads,' said Val, admiring the sharp matt black blade of her machete.

'You're probably wondering what it is you've done to upset me. Let's just say I don't take kindly to anyone mistreating my animals. My animals being the donkeys you nicked. If you'd actually harmed one of them – this'd be a horizontal burial. Without the benefit of a chat.'

'WE WERE ONLY LETTING THEM…' Mary got no further before Val slapped another strip of tape over her lips, cuffing her head with a rough slap for good measure. Mary began to blub.

'Now you've upset me again… If you're not going to upset me again – nod your heads.' Mary and Ian nodded.

93

'*Good boys an' girls!*' Right – I'll see you the day after tomorrow. Don't get any daft ideas about calling for help. If you're not here when I get back then we'll be doing this all over again. Oh and by the way – try and keep your heads still. You don't want to attract any predators.'

'MURGHHH?'

'Hungry foxes and the odd wolf, wild dogs, stoats – ferrets. I'd be more worried about crows and rooks, though. Peck your eyes out, those bastards. Though they do mek nice pets.'

'UHHHH!' groaned Ian.

'Tell you what I could give you,' said Val. 'Couple of pairs of ski goggles, from the van?' Mary and Ian nodded as enthusiastically as they'd ever done for anything in their whole lives.

'Fifty quid a pair,' announced Val, 'you can pay me later as you're not really in a position to cough up any cash just at the moment. You can leave the money with Patrick McCreary in the Fleur de Lys in town. Just don't mek me wait for it. Nod yer 'eads if you understand, boys an' girls.'

★

Val Metcalfe wasn't the only "person of influence" in Whitborough out for justice. Ted Knight had just discovered his pride and joy was missing from the kerb on Rope Walk at the back of his agent's restaurant. The first thing he did, after he calmed down, was to ring his brother-in-law, Superintendent D'Ascoyne, at Whitborough Police Station.

'Ted, let me assure you we will do our utmost to find your car. In fact, I'll make a point of mentioning it to MI5; it might be connected to all the trouble we've been having.'

'MI5 are in Whitborough?'

'You didn't hear me say that.'

'Ahhh. Well if they don't find it in 48 hours – I'm putting Clubland's mafia on it; and believe you me, if they don't find the bastards, nobody will.'

'I hope this won't involve any violence, Ted. I can't be involved in anything like that.'

'Violence? Who said anything about violence...'

'Ted – really, *I don't want to know.*'

'*You're not gonna bloody know.*'

★

In BADCOW headquarters in Burniston the same evening, Mary's absence had been noted for another reason.

'Where's Shipley, Gaz?'

'Gone off in a huff, cos of the dog. Good bloody riddance.'

'She borrowed £2.50 from me for the bus... She's probably in the Headbangers Arms; that's where she usually goes off to sulk. Or in the Three Jolly Morris Men in the village.'

'I thought they'd barred us?'

'Oh yeah – we're barred, *but she ain't.* Her dad's on Whitborough Licensing Committee – and he's in the Masons.'

'Let's lock the doors and pretend we're all in bed!'

Chapter Eighteen

Rock 'n' Roll Damnation.

Inside the market square premises of Clash City Records a small family drama was in progress. News of the Fire Brigade's defeat at the smoking ruin of Mystery City on Rope Walk was just beginning to sink in. After Danny, David Drake's son and Brian's nephew, had revealed the bad news about the fate of the other half of their recently acquired fortune. A fate for which he was solely and entirely responsible. The news was not going down well with his father's brother who had snatched a cavalry sabre from the wall and was pointing it with some venom at his nephew.

'You stupid *IDIOT!'*

'Brian… put the sword down,' said Dave, acidly.

'You *stupid* little bastard…'

'Put the sword down, Uncle Brian, please…'

'PUT THE SWORD DOWN! WHY SHOULD I PUT THE SWORD DOWN?… WHEN I COULD STICK IT IN *YOU!* YOU… STUPID… LITTLE… TWERP!'

'Sorry…'

'SORRY!… SORRY! Is that all you've got to say! You leave half our bloody fortune in gold in a DJ's booth! *A BLOODY DJ'S BOOTH!* A DJ's booth under the care of the biggest psychopath in Whitborough. **MY GOLD!**'

'OUR GOLD!' growled Dave.

'Please Uncle Brian…'

'PLEASE UNCLE BRIAN… PLEASE DON'T STICK ME WITH THE THREE FOOT LONG RAZOR SHARP CAVALRY SABRE… EVEN THOUGH I DESERVE IT,' whined Brian, sarcastically.

'Brian – put the bloody sword down!'

'I'll put the f★★king sword away when this little twit goes down on his hands and knees and BEGS me not to staple his frigging ear to the counter!' spat Brian, slamming the point of the old sword into the scabbard. Only the tip of the sword didn't quite go into the scabbard, because Brian was still shaking with rage.

'BRIAN!'

'What! WHAT?'

'You just stuck the end of that sword in your foot, mate.'

Chapter Nineteen

Carry On Doctor.

PC Jackson Alger woke up in Whitby Hospital with a pounding headache, a throbbing jaw and a strange hummock on his nose – which he presumed must be some sort of protective swathe of wadding and bandages. He was propped up on a padded board, to which he was strapped at an angle halfway between upright and horizontal. Another restraint across his forehead was holding his head to a bracket of some sort fixed to his bed frame. Because of the width of the pad over his nose, and the reams of bandages holding him down, he could see about as much as a medieval knight under a tournament helm, and wondered what sort of injuries he had acquired driving his car into Lazy Jane Lane's boundary hedge to deserve being strapped down like an amputee in Nelson's Navy.

'Don't touch the wadding, Mr Alger, your nose has been reset. Try and breathe through your mouth whilst you're awake, it will help the bone heal faster,' said a kindly, but firm, disembodied voice to his front.

'Who are you – *Where are you?*'

'My name's Nurse Sharpe, Constable. I'm right at the foot of your bed and I'll be here until eight o'clock tonight. Try not to move too much, and don't cough, if you can possibly help it.'

'Why?'

'And if you want to yawn – go easy. You've broken your collarbone and some ribs and fractured your jaw. You're on a bodyboard to stabilise your torso until your bruises go down. If anyone tries to tell you a dirty joke let me know, and I'll have their guts for garters! That's for the benefit of the rest of you...' she added.

'My head's killing me...'

'The ambulance team that brought you in said that you'd broken the front of your radio with the bridge of your nose, Constable. I'm just checking your notes. You can't see me yet because of the wadding the doctor applied. You should be able to see a little of the ward on your left and right sides, but try and rest your eyes as much as you can. Looking out of the side of your vision will give you a headache. Would you like an audiobook? Or I can bring you a radio – but you can't have it on too loud because you'll disturb the other gentlemen.'

'How long am I going to be here?'

'If the doctor's happy you'll be able to go home and convalesce fairly soon, Mr Alger. But it's not my place to say when. As long as you promise not to dig any big trenches in your garden, or go chasing after criminals. And there's plenty on this ward...' she added, sarcastically.

'God – what a mess...' groaned Alger pitifully, 'is there a Mr Kingcombe in here? Dudley Kingcombe?'

'There was a gentleman by that name who came in with you. But he had his thumb reset then he went home. Though I think he might have popped back briefly to leave a card for Mr Gall.'

'Home to Devon?'

'I don't know, sir. I don't expect we'll need to see him again. Matron said he left in a bit of a hurry.'

'What time is it, Nurse?'

'Four o'clock – would you like something to eat?'

'FOUR O'CLOCK!'

'There's a glass of water on the table beside you with a straw next to it.'

'Four o'clock... I've never slept that long in years.'

'I expect you'd be raring to go by now if you weren't in here. But we have to make the best of what life throws our way, sir, so try not to get yourself excited.' Alger sensed the nurse close to his ear and gulped, expecting her to stick a needle in his arm. But all she did was whisper in his ear. 'If you need to go, Mr Alger, there's an on-call button taped to your finger – just press it with your thumb, I'll come over with a bottle and we'll whip the curtains out. Doctor decided not to catheterise you whilst you're still mobile.'

'MOBILE? *How am I mobile?*'

'The webbing straps are just a precaution, Mr Alger – whilst you were sedated. We can undo the straps tomorrow once everything settles down, and we make sure you haven't bruised yourself on the inside. Spleens can be tricky things, dear... you've had a lucky escape...'

'I don't feel lucky. I feel like shit,' he added miserably.

'We've got gloves and scrubs for everything, sir. Including that. Will there be anything else?'

'Did you say Mr Gall was in here, Nurse?'

'Albert? He's on the opposite side of the ward, Mr Alger, right in front of you. But you'll not be seeing much of him yet, sir. He's been sedated again today. It's been a bit of a night for ribs; though if he hadn't had the foresight to jam a nice thick pet bed between his chest and his Land Rover's steering wheel I dare say the poor love would have had a sheet over his head. But you didn't hear that from me. He's got the best set of black eyes I've seen since Henry Cooper and Muhammed Ali knocked seven bells out of each other. If Mr Gall keeps you awake at night groaning just call the duty nurse with your button and she'll bring you some ear plugs.'

Then a young boy on the opposite side of the ward, next to Albert, called to Nurse Sharpe.

'Nursey?'

'Yes, Mark?'

'Nurse, that man – Mr Gall, he's growing furry.'

'You've been reading that comic for hours, Mark Day. I think it's time you rested your eyes. It's not polite to stare at people when they're asleep.'

'He wasn't that hairy yesterday, Nurse. Look at his arms.'

'Why, pray, should I look at Mr Gall's arms, young man?'

'Because!'

'If I look at Mr Gall's arms will you promise me you'll go to sleep until seven?'

'All right! I promise. You have to look at his feet, too.'

'Mark! Stop it. I will NOT be looking at Mr Gall's feet. Mr Gall is not in here for his feet. All Mr Gall's problems are above the waist.'

'But he's got furry in other places – and his toe nails are gross – and he growls in his sleep. His face went all funny last night when you turned the lights off. He's scaring me…'

'**YOU** – are a bad young man… Mr Gall can't go anywhere right now because he's strapped to his bed and he's full of medicine to make him sleep.'

'Nurse Sharpe – can I call you Alex?'

'You can call me Alexandra – but only when you whisper to me.'

'You promised to look!'

'All right… I'm looking now… Oh my goodness! That is odd.'

'See, I told you!'

'Mark… have you done this to Mr Gall?' asked Nurse Sharpe, pointing at Albert's limp palm.

'Done what, Nurse?'

'Have you stuck all these hairs from the floor on his palms with that tube of glue your mum gave you for your models? What a rotten thing to do! I'm certainly not going to go rolling up his pyjamas and see what you've done to the rest of him. **NOW GO TO SLEEP**.'

Chapter Twenty

The Sword in the Scholl.

In Clash City Records not even a self-inflicted stabbing was going to stop the Drake brothers making a sale. Two of their best customers had just come in, after their weekly paydays, to buy a couple of bullet belts and two Ozzy Osbourne t-shirts. But Brian was still standing in the middle of the shop with the point of his sabre stuck in his foot, trying his very best to look nonchalant.

'I hope the bullet belts fit, lads. It took us a while to get those...They're hard to find in chrome.'

'These are ace, Brian. Just what we was after.'

'Yeah, the Blizzard of Ozz t-shirts are pretty cool for bootlegs. I might come back for another next week.'

'We got plenty – haven't we, Dave,' said Brian, tautly.

'Aye – all free of bloodstains,' smirked his brother, trying to control himself whilst he took their customers' money.

'Brian... is that a real sword in your foot?' asked one of the young men, as they took their carrier bags and change from his giggling brother.

'Yes, nothing for you to worry about, lads, just a little accident.'

'Are you going to pull it out?'

'Oh – no hurry. I just thought I'd wait a minute until you'd got your belts and t-shirts…'

'Can we watch?'

'Watch what?'

'Can we watch you pull it out? I've never seen a knife wound.'

'Lads – thanks very much for your custom, but I don't think my brother wants an audience right now,' smiled Dave. 'He's in a bit of pain – as you can see.'

'Please, Brian… we won't tell anyone. Promise…'

'Thanks for your concern, lads, but it might be bloody,' explained Brian, gritting his teeth as another spasm of agony suddenly got his attention.

'Oh don't worry, Bri mate, we don't mind a bit of blood.'

'Lads… you need to leave now – really. Does it hurt, Brian?'

'**YES**… it friggin hurts. Can somebody get me some painkillers, please?'

'I could get some for you?'

'No… really.'

'Roy's training to be a nurse, Brian… aren't you, Roy?'

'Oh yeah… I've done all me first aid. Dressings and stitches, medication. I could have a look at it for you and clean it up. Bandage it until you get to A&E.'

'A&E?'

'Accident and Emergency, Brian, you'll have to get a doctor to look at that, you know.'

'Can someone get me some bloody painkillers, *PLEASE!*'

'I'll get Dean up, he can go,' suggested Dave.

'But we'll have to shut the record department…'

'Just for a few minutes, Bri…'

'You should sit down on a chair, Brian, it'll help take the pressure off your foot and slow the blood loss, and you won't fall down if you faint,' advised Roy, the trainee nurse. 'When the sword comes out you need to elevate your foot and put some pressure on the hole with a clean cloth. There'll probably be a bit of blood squirting out but if you put pressure on it, it won't be so bad.'

'Oh thanks – thanks a lot…'

'No problem, mate. Have you got a first aid kit – an' some antiseptic?'

'Dave – have we got a first aid kit?'

'Why would we have a first aid kit?'

Dave picked up the intercom and called their senior sales assistant, Dean Beadle, in the cellar. 'Beadle – get your arse upstairs. Brian's stabbed himself.'

'You what!'

'Brian has stabbed himself. We need you to go to Boyes and buy some bandages and stuff.'

'Where's he stabbed himself?'

'In my foot,' growled Brian.

'Ha ha haaaaaaaaaaa…'

'If you don't get yourself up here right now I'm going to ask for my Motorhead ticket back, Beadle.'

'On me way!'

Chapter Twenty-One

Dirty Deeds, Done Dead Cheap.

In their room at The Brontes Guest House on Long Acre, the two MACE MI5 agents began to analyse the progress they had made and exchange their theories on their assignment before leaving their room for dinner.

'What were your first impressions of our brothers in arms, Bruce?'

'I'd say they were as uncomfortable with us as they are with this case. I'd say their Chief doesn't trust us one iota. Mr D'Ascoyne – is going to need a bit of work. The Royal Navy are playing along, and the Home Office are trying to please the Home Secretary who's trying his damnedest to get a result to save his career. I'd say none of them have got any idea what's really going on and they're not going to put any skin in the game until we come up with a good lead or a prisoner. That Inspector – Marshall – and his Sergeant are smart enough; they're the ones we should be shadowing, sir. Plenty of savvy and local knowledge. That's where we'll get our break, or the clue we need to crack this open.'

'Yes, that's my analysis. Then it's time we improved our odds and engaged in a little eavesdropping. Mr Marshall's home address and car will be a good place to start; we'll do his Sergeant's, too. Then their office at the station. You can put shielded passive mikes in Marshall and Broadhead's office. Another in the gents'– under the bottom of the urinal on the drain pipe coupling – and another behind the coffee machine at the top of the stairs at the back of the station. Shouldn't take you too long.'

'I've already miked Marshall's house, sir. There's a camera too – overlooking the door inside.'

'Good work. I've hired a motorhome for us. MACE budgets are a little more generous so we're going to be eavesdropping in comfort instead of getting a numb backside in the back of a van. Control is sending us two reliefs from the new intake. So we can be round the clock. Six-hour shifts for three days, or longer if necessary.'

'Their station office could be a bit tricky, sir. That corridor there is pretty busy.'

'There's a switchboard cupboard right next door to Marshall's office. I had a look at the building plans and the blueprints of the station before we left London. There's a service panel at the bottom of the wall between the two rooms, and you can get into his office through that; close their blinds then plant the bugs, and leave from the switchboard cupboard. It won't matter if anyone sees you. They know we're doing regular security sweeps inside and they all know our faces.'

'There's nothing blocking the panel on his side is there, sir?'

'If there is you'll have to move it, Bruce.'

'I noticed there was a bookshelf under the whiteboard on that wall when D'Ascoyne gave us the tour.'

'Grey-green with a sloping metal tray?'

'Yes sir – how did…'

'Same as the MOD. Don't worry – they're on castors. One good shove and you're in.'

'All right, sir. I'll get on it. What are you doing tomorrow?'

'I'm going to our house in LS2.'

'Leeds?'

'Mmm. Progress report then a couple of interviews, and a release. We took custody of a reporter from the York Evening Press from the police. They nabbed him inside their C.S tape at Carr Wold Parkway, digging for dirt. Though he didn't exactly get what he came for. He fell in a skip and knocked himself out. The crafty bastard had a disguise to pass himself off as a cleaning company delivery driver. Shows a certain dedication to the craft.'

'The craft of what – espionage?'

'Journalism. He's probably got delusions of joining the *World in Action* team.'

'What was he doing there?'

'Trying to get some audio on the Mexican bum fight.'

'AHHH! He's not a tongue for the Russians then?'

'No. A bedsit Ernesto Guevara is probably the best description of Mr Crawford. We've been giving him the works and making him sweat. But sweat is about all we've got out of him. Sweat and a few juicy tit-bits about the private lives of York's Communist Party. It's time to let him go home, and wash the lasagne off his shirt. But I'm more interested in the teacher we've got, the one that set off the old cannon in the Sea Cadet's parade ground – that is if his hearing's come back. Should be an interesting conversation. I've got someone from the bomb squad to speak to, as well, about those Luftwaffe bombs. They didn't fall from the sky. They were buried there. They must have come from that cache of arms Marshall mentioned in the briefing before D'Ascoyne suspended him.'

'From that farming family, the Hoopers…'

'His mate Broadhead took out all the files on that bunch recently.'

'Doesn't sound like a coincidence?'

'I think he's copying the files for Marshall.'

Chapter Twenty-Two

I'll Be the Ticket – If You're My Inspector.

By four o'clock on Friday afternoon, Whitborough Borough Council's deadliest traffic warden, Violet Penrose, had ticketed a grand total of nineteen cars and vans in her allotted sector; from Kenwith Valley Gorge and Foreshore Road to the bent and twisted streets of Whitborough's old town beyond the back of the Market Hall.

Sixteen of the victims on her guilty tally were business vehicles and delivery trucks overstaying their unloading times. But Violet had also caught Mel Hazzard's Porsche 911 on the slipway outside the Newcastle Packet, heaped more misery on the unfortunate owner of an Austin Allegro that had broken down on the cobbles of Badd Lane, and caught the driver of a forlorn old MGB GT asleep on the front concourse of the Futurama Cinema.

Violet had just an hour left in which to reach her milestone hundredth weekly ticket – and claim her Wheaton's hamper from the council's bonus scheme to add to her exceptional service award. She was looking forward to being the first warden in the borough to reach the hundred, and could barely contain her excitement at the prospect of buttressing her daunting reputation with a record tally.

Roy Rudd – the Black Hand Coven's own Aleister Crowley – was the only other traffic warden who had ever come close to making a century during their normal 39-hour working week, with ninety-six undisputed fines in the last quarter of July, 1981. Though his record was remembered as much for the accident that had ended his ambitions as his near miss.

Roy's run of good fortune had come to an abrupt end, whilst he was writing his ninety-seventh ticket outside the Rowing Club, when an oar-cleat attached to a small yawl that was being towed away hooked his trouser pocket and he was dragged screaming down the foreshore by his Marks & Spencer's slacks to the Toll Booth junction. His ordeal only ended when the owner of the Toyota Land Cruiser, towing the boat noticed a bare leg under the shredded remains of a pair of black trousers in his wing mirror. The overlocking on his pocket had lasted all the way up to third gear before the cleat had moved into the leg of his Y-fronts; inflicting a Chinese burn to the pale flesh of his inside thigh which no amount of antiseptic cream would ever be able to cool.

Mindful of her rival's untimely accident, and deeply superstitious as all good witches should be, Violet decided not to take any unecessary risks on her quest for her final ticket. She knew that her best chance for success lay on the flagstone pavements in front of the road to the fish quay where visitors stopped to use the old toilets.

It was ten pence to spend a penny in the magnificently appointed Victorian bath house and WC, and only a ten pence piece could open the doors of the cubicles, so anyone without the correct change was forced to visit one of the small shops or kiosks nearby before they could get any sort of relief. This almost guaranteed they would overstay the maximum loading and unloading time on the pavement. So Violet crossed the road – and stood nonchalantly in the lee of the doors to the RNLI building – to blend in with the crowds whilst she waited to pounce.

Within a few minutes an opportunity presented itself in the form of a blue Lambretta 150, carrying two young men wearing two-tone suits under fishtail parkas, that drew up against the kerb, revved the engine and mounted the pavement, to let the ambulance that was speeding towards Brian Drake's speared foot get past. The passenger dismounted and removed his helmet, followed by the rider who put the scooter on its stand, turned off the engine and engaged the steering lock.

Violet looked at the second hand on her wristwatch, checking the time against the clock face on the tower above the harbourmaster's office, and then took a quick swig of gin, from the perfume bottle she kept in her handbag, as a fortifying tonic before moving off.

Violet scented blood and took out her ticketbook, moving slowly towards the scooter as the two boys ambled off unhurriedly to the toilets. They were already forty seconds into their stay before they had even moved off. Though Violet wasn't allowed to write a ticket until a parking infringement had already been committed, she was already poised to strike; but she had to be careful. The owners of the shops and kiosks on the fish quay hated the wardens preying on visitors and tourists who were potential customers, and were ruthless in reporting any over-zealous enforcement of the regulations that risked antagonising anyone browsing their stalls.

Violet checked her watch again just as the boys found the door to the gents' after negotiating a crowd of retired couples striding back from a turn around the harbour. Their clock was ticking towards one minute and thirty seconds. Another ten seconds passed before the lads re-emerged and walked off in opposite directions following a brief examination of their wallets.

Violet took a deep breath, smirked triumphantly, and returned to the Lambretta. She made a show of inspecting the machine for another minute, then ticketed the scooter and was striding back across Foreshore Road with a spring in her step when a black Ford Capri drew up at the kerb and a familiar face leant out of the driver's side window. It was none other than Ronnie Gould, the Black Hand Coven's very own hairdresser and entertainment officer, their "Comte de St Germain".

'Oooh, you do look good in uniform, Vi,' he purred.

'Watch it, Larry, (Ronnie's nickname – the first name of camp TV host, Larry Grayson) I'm still on duty. I'll give you a ticket an' all.'

'Have you upset somebody, Vi?'

'Probably. Why?'

'There are a couple of scooterists waving a ticket at you on the other pavement.'

'Open your passenger door – you can give me a lift to the office. I'm nearly ready to clock off.' Violet stepped into the passenger seat and closed the door as Ronald re-joined the traffic, and then performed a U-turn, coming to a stop right beside the two mods that Violet had so grievously offended.

'Thanks for the ticket, you sneaky cow!' snarled the rider, taking a step towards the side of the Capri. 'You can stick your ticket up your arse,' he growled, crushing the cover sheet of Violet's ticket up into a ball before throwing it at the wing of Ronald's car.

'Do you want a curse with that too?' said Violet, menacingly, showing off her teeth with a very wide smile.

'WHAT!'

'I'm a witch, as well as a warden, sonny. So if you don't want seven years of bad luck and trouble you better pick my ticket up and keep it safe. **Or you'll be in shit up to your eyeballs – until I make your hair fall out... UNDERSTAND?** Have a nice weekend now...' she said, smiling wickedly, as Ronald floored the accelerator of the Capri, leaving the speechless scooterists choking in a cloud of petrol fumes.

'I thought I might find you by the Lifeboat, Vi,' said Ronald, shifting into third as they picked up speed.

'Did you now?'

'Do you want to fasten your seatbelt?'

'No, I don't. It'll crease me uniform.'

'Suit yourself.'

'I always do.'

'I came to find you because our great leader, Derek, has asked me to get in touch with everybody. I tried to ring you this morning from the salon, but you must have left for work. So I thought I'd come and find you when Tony got in – just to get away from the fumes. Everyone wants their hair done on a Friday. I'd done three tints, four perms, four grade ones, two tidy-ups and a colouring before Tony came in. That's how mad it's been. I was on my bloody knees, Vi.'

'You can do mine tomorrow. On your knees, or standing up, I couldn't care less as long as it's done.'

'If you can get in early enough – I'll see what we can do.'

'I'll be most upset if you can't,' said Violet, examining the thin pincers of her favourite tweezers. 'So what does his majesty want?' she said airily.

'He said he wants to speak to us all informally so I suggested we should all go out for a quiet few drinks tomorrow night, then he can get round everybody individually while we're all together.'

'I wonder what it is this time?' said Violet, without any hint of enthusiasm.

'I'm not sure. But I think he's a little peeved at the state of the Golden Dawn papers you sent back to him.'

'Can't do a little magic without breaking a few eggs.'

'I don't think he found any egg on his precious manuscript, Violet. It was the pesto and curry sauce stains that he took exception to. You've stained the sacred Tree of Life, dear.'

'So what? I like to eat while I'm studying. Nothing wrong with that. Fingerprints and smears – all part of a document's history, ain't they? It's got some of my history on it now,' she smirked. 'So where are we meeting?'

'Well, Derek said he can't get out until after half past eight so I spoke to Maureen and suggested we meet up in the snug at the Jack. Derek said he'll meet us in the Dickens and we can spend the rest of the night in there.'

'Is Phyllis going to be there…?' asked Violet – reaching down for his copy of the Whitborough Evening News in the passenger footwell.

'I don't know, pet. Have you seen the front page there?'

'No I hadn't – and don't call me pet.'

'Something's kicked off in Kettleness.'

'Oh…?'

'It's just above Whitby.'

'Yes, I know where it is,' said Violet, her eyes fixed on the front page.

'Are you all right, Vi?'

'Someone just walked over me grave, Ron,' muttered Violet, staring intently at the opening columns and the photograph of a Land Rover on its side in a large pond. 'DEATH AND DESTRUCTION IN KETTLENESS,' screamed the banner headline, over three dramatically italicised sub-headings: *FORMER SOLDIER INTERVIEWED – DETECTIVES QUESTION LOCAL FARMER – STRANGE WILD ANIMAL ON THE LOOSE.*

'*WILD ANIMAL ON THE LOOSE?*' scoffed Violet. 'Is there any other kind?'

'I think they meant anything that isn't a sheep.'

'Been polishing your wit have you, Ron?'

'It sounds quite interesting. I don't usually buy the paper.'

'Oh it's interesting all right – you can take me home now.'

'I thought you wanted to get back to your office?'

'Oh, they can wait 'til Monday.'

'If you're sure.'

'I am.'

'Aren't you supposed to leave your uniform and your ticket book at the council's office?'

'Only if I get back in time before it closes. They won't say nothing to my face anyhow.'

'Oh – why?'

'Because they're terrified of me. Do you want a mint?'

Chapter Twenty-Three

Mrs Valhalla–Goes to Town.

Elsie Cakebread, co-owner of Valhalla Retirement Home with her business partner and husband "Big" Mark Ellis, was having a late afternoon coffee with her friend, Audrey Holliday, at Crooklands Cafe on Ramsgill High Street.

'You all shopped out then, Else?' asked Audrey, glancing at the mound of carrier bags arranged around Elsie's biker boots.

'Aye, just a few bits and bobs. Mark asked me to go to the post office to get a few hundred quid in francs and gilders. Then I had to go to Woolworths to the Photo-Me booth.'

'Oh... nice.'

'I need to get me passport renewed. We're off to Assen this summer to see the Grand Prix. We're tekking some of our lot from Valhalla in the minibus. Overnight ferry from Hull on the Thursday, back on the Monday.'

'Who's looking after things while you're away?'

'Oh the rest of 'em should be all right on their own. They've got the key codes for the bar and the keys to the gun cabinet. They'll be reet,' she sighed, 'they'll just have one rock club to go to now instead of two. Have you seen the state of Mystery City? It looks like a bomb site in Lebanon. I thought the bloody world was coming to an end with an earthquake when it blew up. Whitborough's like a bloody war-zone at the moment – I can't help thinking, what's going to happen next?'

'Oh I know, pet. I hope it isn't going to put off the tourists. Our little museum would die a death. I thought it were an earthquake, too. We lost a litre of water from the fish after a bloody tidal wave in the tank when that blast shook the 'ouse. Me poor little fish have been hiding in the crevices of Atlantis ever since. Where's this Assen place?'

'Holland.'

'Holland?'

'What's Atlantis?'

'Oh it's just what we call the resin ruin we bought to put in the fish tank. Looks a bit like a piece of that Glastonbury Abbey, after Henry the Eighth had wrecked it.'

'I'm her Eighth old man I'm 'ennery… Wouldn't have a Willy or a Sam!'

'HA! Been in the knife drawer, Else!'

'Aye, well, I've got to have me wits about me at our place. Back to the subject of our holiday – the beer's bloody lovely in Assen. A lot better than the shit they serve round here. There's a great big party on the Friday, so we'll be having a blowout and an armful o' Dutch pastries. Then we'll have two days to settle our 'eads and sit n' watch Sheeney and Roberts and Spencer. God, I love the smell of two-strokes on a morning.'

'What's a two-stroke?'

'It's a type of petrol engine, Aud, like the one that runs your mower, only these ones are a bit noisier. They smoke a bit, too, but they smell grand.'

'Well, each to their own.'

'So what brings you into town, girl?'

'Oh this and that... I went to Jemima's to get my hair done. *As you can see.* D'you like it? It's called Midnight Cranberry,' said Audrey, tilting her head back for inspection.

'It looks ace, pet. Classy...'

'Oh thanks, Else... I can always depend on you. I said to Jemima – I want to look like Joan Jett – but with a bit more length... like Elvira. But layered to give it a bit of lift... like Debbie Harry has 'ers... but not too tarty, like Joan Collins.'

'Is Joan Collins tarty? I always thought she were quite classy.'

'She were a right tart in *The Bitch.*'

'She does play a good bitch.'

'She's had a few, hasn't she...'

'Audrey! Shush!'

'I mean she's had a few 'usbands, like that other one over there in Hollywood who's always in the papers – the one with the funny name – Zsa Zsa Gosfort. The serial wotsit – y'know.'

'Actress?'

'No.'

'Divorcee?'

'That an' all.'

'Isn't Gosfort in Newcastle, Aud?'

'Gosfort – listen to me, I meant Zsa Zsa Gabor. Just give me a slap. Gosfort, blummin 'eck the things that come out o' my mouth when I'm not looking. God – I wish I 'ad just one of the bloody diamonds that cow's been bought. One o' them rocks would set me up for the rest of me bleeding life. I could be a lady of leisure. Instead of wasting my life working in that bloody museum. The only things in there that ain't already dead are as gay as Larry Grayson. I've got as much chance of finding a rich fella in there as a bloody shire horse has of winning the Grand National.'

'You never told me Alan was gay.'

'It's practically compulsory in the Kenwith Valley Gorge Museum. There's more bum groping going on in that blumming archiving room than in a series of *I Claudius*. The only trouble is, it's not my cheeks getting pinched…' she said wistfully, 'the things I could do with Robert Mitchum…'

'They're never at it at work, Aud!'

'Huh! Let's just say it's a good idea to knock loudly before you go into the archive rooms.'

'Well at least they leave you alone. I didn't know you were sweet on Robert Mitchum.'

'Wouldn't you?'

'He has got a nice voice.'

'He's just so – so masculine – in that old fashioned way.'

'Oh yeah – in an old fashioned way. Old school.'

'God, I just melt when I see him in one of them big overcoats. Robert PHWOARRR! In *The Winds of War*!'

'Oh I remember that. That mini-series, on the telly. ITV, weren't it? So is there no-one who takes your fancy at the Museum?'

'There's a nice fella on the Board of Directors, might be promising.'

'Aren't they all getting on a bit?'

'I wouldn't mind, actually, if he were just a teensy bit more good looking. I could do with cheering up. There's been a bit of a funny atmosphere at work at the moment, even the flirty comments have tailed off – Alan's a bit on edge. It just feels different, I don't know. If I'm being honest the place feels a bit creepy. I feel like I'm being watched… I can't put me finger on it. Maybe it's just me.'

'Are you feeling all right?'

'Oh yeah, I feel completely different when I'm not at work. I'd go back to the theatre in a flash, but they never gave me enough hours and I'd be back working every weekend – I like having it off – *the weekends I mean.*'

'Maybe it'll pass.'

'Maybe.'

'Hey! You're not going through the change, are you?'

'You cheeky cow! I'm not that bloody old!'

'Well, I'd better get back to the madhouse and put our holiday money in the safe. I hate the thought I might lose it. Even if it is funny money.'

'Do you want an escort, Else?'

'Aye, that'd be nice – you can give me a hand with all me bags. Let's have another coffee first, though, I'm gagging for some more caffeine. **Can we have another two coffees, luv?'** shouted Elsie, waving a menu at the girl behind the counter.

'Did any of your lot see that ship blow up in Vicky Bay?'

'No. But I think we probably heard it… We was all on the terrace watching the Easter meeting. Mark brought the jukebox out on the extension lead. I 'eard a bang but I didn't think owt of it at the time. Thought it were probably someone blowing their bike up on Gunstone pulling wheelies or summat. Did you see it?'

'No. I was in the back garden on me sun lounger. I heard a rumble. But I thought it were thunder. Until all the sirens

121

started. The Mayor and the Mayoress were on that helicopter, y'know.'

'Helicopter?'

'The one with the ship. Blown to bits it were.'

'Oh dear… that's a shame… from first citizen of the borough to fish food. The bastard came through y'know. When I had me last seance.'

'What! The Mayor?'

'Aye, the one an' only. Then I had that bloke from Zombieland Video.'

'You've had a right time of it, girl.'

'Don't I know it… I'm not sure if it wasn't too much for the spiritualists; they're quite a delicate lot. They were probably hoping for Lawrence of Arabia – or Joan of Arc – an' all they got was a fat fraudster and a lewd old git from Scotland. They're letting any old Tom, Dick or Harry into the lower astral planes these days.'

'Are you having another circle this week, then?'

'Not bloody likely. I'm having a rest. You should see what the last one did to me blummin' eggs.'

'Eh?'

'Me Faberge eggs. You know, the ones I keep on the glass shelves in the Gold Cup lounge. Genuine reproductions they was! Limited editions from the *Sunday Mirror* magazine. Mark bought 'em for me – for our anniversary. A hundred and fifty quids' worth… ruined. We had to have the carpet shampooed an' all. All cos some silly cow from the Spiritualist Church puked up on the tablecloth and the floor – that were before she cracked 'er toenail. Apparently I were channelling 'er husband, Mr Zombieland – 'til Stuart came in and ruined everything – couldn't bloody wait 'alf an hour for me to change over the bloody Guinness, could he. Funny thing is, the rest of the Spiritualists said she weren't using 'er married name when she signed up to come over with them. Summat fishy going on. On top of all that Mark's not been speaking to me since I made him screw Agostini, Mike Hailwood and Alice Cooper to the wall.'

'You made him do what?!'

'They all needed it... they've been getting tossed off all over the couch – when I was getting it on with the guests.'

'*Getting it on?*'

'Well, you know me, I do take pride in keeping a happy house. I've bent over backwards for those twats in the Town Hall.'

'I truly admire someone who can do all the things you do, Elsie, and then have the guts to confess it all to people like me.'

'Isla. That was 'er name. Isla?'

'Who?'

'That hard-faced old cow that came with the Spiritualists. I should have known she were no good.'

'Isla? I only know one Isla in Whitborough. Isla Binnie, her husband's that Tony. Tony Binnie – Mr Zombieland. Zombieland Video. That bloke you said you had processed – possessed you. They got mixed up with that other lot from the old Isadora Duncan Free Dance Society. I'll tell you one thing, it ain't a dance society no more.'

'Oh...?'

'Let's just say you'd be wise to keep your distance from that lot.'

'They're into murder and child slavery, are they, Aud?'

'Worse than that... Ever seen that film – *Rosemary's Baby*? About Satanists?'

'Satanists? Don't be daft.'

'I'm telling you straight. They're devil worshippers.'

'Devil worshippers? Devil worshippers! HUH! That's the last time she's getting her feet under my bloody table.'

Chapter Twenty-Four

Scary Movie.

Inside the second floor corridor of Whitborough Police Station a flustered Superintendent D'Ascoyne was on the warpath, searching the back offices for Detective Sergeant Broadhead. But DS Broadhead was three floors below in "Barry's bunker" – the stores, records and evidence room in the bowels of the station – signing out the spare copy of the mysterious video recording from the camera in the front foyer.

'You watching that here, George?' asked Sergeant Whitefield.

'Aye, if the set's working.'

'Are you sure you want to see this?'

'What d'you mean?'

'You know that's the tape with *the thing* on it, do you?'

'Thing?'

'The ghost thing.'

'And?'

'All right George, don't say I didn't warn you. Your Inspector Marshall's got the other one. This is the only other copy.'

'So what's the crack with this? Ray says it's a bit out of the ordinary.'

'Out of the ordinary? There's an understatement…'

'You've seen it then?'

'Yep. I wish I never seen the damn tape. I'll tell you that for free, George.'

'So why is it so scary?'

'Just take the bloody thing out my sight, George. It gives me the bloody creeps just handling it.'

'All right.'

'And do me a favour – once you've seen it – lose it somewhere, will you?'

'Where's Broadhead?'

'In Mr Marshall's office, sir?'

'If you don't know, say so.'

'I don't rightly know, sir…'

'And?'

'And what, sir?'

'When was the last time you saw him, Constable?'

'In the canteen, sir, getting a coffee from the machine.'

'Did he go up or down?'

'Sir?'

'Did he go *upstairs* or *downstairs*?'

'I don't know, sir.'

'If you see him send him straight to my office, Steadman. Straight away.'

'Yes, sir!'

'Just one other thing… have the gentlemen from London asked to speak to you about anything yet? The two men from MI5?

'Not yet, sir.'

'Oh. Do you know if they've seen Inspector Marshall yet?'

'I couldn't say, sir.'

'Okay, well…'

'They've got Constable Elland in the interview room at the moment, sir.'

'Have they? Good, good.'

'Yes, sir.'

'Has Dodds had any success locating Mr Knight's stolen Mercedes saloon?'

'Not yet, sir.'

'I want to be informed the moment it's found.'

'Yes, sir.'

'Carry on.'

Broadhead, in the habit of the older, wiser policemen in Whitborough, always used the staircase at the northern end of the police station and never used the lifts. This cunning strategy served a dual purpose for Broadhead, giving him one of his few opportunities for exercise whilst keeping him far away from his superiors. It was this route he used to return to the office he shared with his suspended colleague Inspector Marshall, to watch the surveillance tape on their shared television and video unit. At the top of the staircase there was a large hot drinks machine and a Police Federation display tower neatly concealing the sliding door to the utility and meters cupboard. A cupboard which had saved many a PC from bumping into their superiors. Broadhead checked the frosted glass wall for any sign of the tell-tale black chequerboard hat, beloved by his Superintendent, before stopping outside the corridor to get himself a cup of instant coffee. Within a couple of minutes he was safely enclosed within the office he shared with Inspector Marshall, with the blinds closed and the lights off. He pushed the cassette into the video recorder and leaned back into his chair.

Nothing out of the ordinary appeared on the tape recording, and after a few minutes Broadhead pressed the stop and eject buttons and took it out. There was a small white blob of Tippex a third of the way into the tape spool window so he re-inserted it, pressed fast forward for ten seconds and then pressed stop. He ejected the tape again and saw that the edge of the remaining spool was now almost level with the white mark in the window so he re-inserted the tape and pressed play, while finishing off his coffee. The television picture showed a wide-angle view of the reception area on Mallory Parade with the three-quarter height counter partition on the extreme left of the screen. The bottom third of the lower screen showed the floor and the small public bench, and the upper portion displayed the walls and skirting to the top of the main door frame. Car headlight beams bleached out the textures of road and pavements, periodically, as the late-night traffic crawled past the police station, outside the full-length glass windows.

Broadhead yawned and glanced over at the photocopier, as it churned out the Hooper family records file, keeping his other eye on the television. A girl with shoulder length blonde hair, wearing a light Barbour-style mac, came in and stood in front of the desk holding a large buff-coloured envelope, which she passed to the clerk through the aperture under the window. After a short conversation she turned around, re-adjusted her handbag strap and then stepped towards the door to leave. What happened next made Boldwood glad he had already finished drinking his coffee.

The girl suddenly dropped her handbag and dashed towards the bottom right-hand corner of the picture; then the street lamp outside went out. Broadhead craned forward, squinting, just as the reception area doors blew in and the downlights in the lobby dimmed. Then suddenly Superintendent D'Ascoyne opened his office door and strode inside, stopping in front of Inspector Marshall's desk.

'Ah! Sergeant Broadhead, I'd like to have a word with you please, in my office,' said D'Ascoyne, fidgeting with the order of some papers he was holding.

'Is that our lobby?' asked D'Ascoyne, suddenly distracted by the scene playing out on the television.

'Yes, sir.'

'And how is this tape recording related to our primary case exactly?'

'I might be in a position to answer your question once I've actually watched it, sir.'

'What – on – earth is that?'

The grainy, black and white recording did nothing to lessen the impact of what had come into the frame; a tall, indistinct and featureless human form, wreathed in a cloak of fog, which seemed to have a life all of its own, moved jerkily towards the clerk's window. Then a leather folder falls to the floor from the right side of the black shadowy form as the tallest portion of the figure suddenly detaches and flies up towards the camera lens. The screen suddenly goes black, and the lid on a huge bloodstained eye opens before fading into darkness. Suddenly the picture is restored and the girl dashes out through the open doors as the street lamp suddenly comes back to life.

'Blimey…' whispered the detective, letting the pencil he was chewing drop from his lip into his lap.

'Sergeant Broadhead, much as I respect your record and dedication, I shouldn't need to impress on you how inappropriate it is to be watching homemade horror films when you're on duty.'

'Sir – this is footage from our CCTV camera in reception. I've just signed it out from records and evidence…'

'From *our* camera in reception?'

'Did you want to see me about something, sir?'

'It can wait… I think… Yes – errr… another time perhaps, Sergeant. Carry on…'

'Yes, sir. It takes your breath away a bit, doesn't it? Shall I rewind it so you can see it ag…'

'Carry on, Broadhead,' stammered D'Ascoyne, almost tripping over the wastepaper basket in his haste to get away from the television and out of Marshall's office.

'Bugger me… I think I might watch that again,' said Broadhead.

Superintendent D'Ascoyne made it to his office and closed the door; then rushed into the small adjoining washroom, ran the cold tap over the basin and splashed his face with cold water. After a few minutes staring anxiously at himself in the mirror, he left the bathroom and poured himself a large Scotch. Ever since he could remember he had been terrified of anything to do with ghosts. He had just swallowed his Johnnie Walker in two gulps when there was a knock at the door.

'Superintendent?'

'COME!' replied D'Ascoyne tetchily, patting his face with a clean handkerchief. 'Agent Keogh? An unexpected – visit… how may we help with your enquiries?' he asked, careful not to show too much warmth.

'Are you all right, Superintendent?' enquired the agent with genuine concern.

'I'm perfectly fine. What do you want?'

'Sir… Captain Stocke, my colleague, would like to speak to you, sir, in the interview room, if you please?'

'My interview room, do you mean?'

'The joint services room, sir.'

'What's this about?'

'The joint investigation, sir.'

'Does this concern any particular individual?' asked D'Ascoyne, trying to sound disinterested.

'Inspector Marshall, sir. Are you sure you're quite well, sir – you look very pale.'

'I've just told you… *I'm fine…*' replied D'Ascoyne, acidly. 'Captain Stocke wishes to see me now?'

'Yes, sir.'

'Give me five minutes,' he answered warily. 'And who else is attending, may I ask?'

'Just yourself and Captain Stocke, sir.'

'Just us.'

'Sir.'

'Tell Captain Stocke I'll be there asap. Was there something else?' asked D'Ascoyne, as the MI5 officer remained standing, legs spread, his right hand holding his wrist in front of his hips in the classic stance favoured by bodyguards the world over.

'I'm to escort you, sir.'

'Are you indeed?'

'Yes, sir.'

'And what if I was to say I don't wish to come unless I have a formal written invitation and a witness?'

'We would have to accommodate you, sir, but unfortunately time is of the essence. May I say it is in your best interests and advantage to attend.'

'You people would say that, wouldn't you. Tell your Captain I'll be down in a minute.'

'I am to escort you, sir.'

'On whose authority?'

'The Home Secretary, sir.'

'I will be confirming all this with the Chief Constable, Mr Keogh.'

'As you wish, sir.'

'You have rank, presumably. In MI5?'

'Captain Stocke is my superior, sir. But we all work for the same boss, sir.'

'Just remember this is my station, Mr Keogh.'

'Yes sir. I'm just following orders, sir. I don't mean any disrespect. We'd be very grateful if you'd come straight away, sir, there's been a new development... that's as much as I can say...'

'Has there... is it about the missing Mercedes?'

'Missing Mercedes?'

Five minutes later, Superintendent D'Ascoyne entered the temporary joint services conference room in his station to meet Captain Stocke; although he had left his tunic in the wardrobe in his office, he had made a point of putting on his hat.

'Superintendent.'

'Captain Stocke.'

'Thank you for coming, Superintendent.'

'I didn't think I had a choice. I am aware of my rights to have a witness.'

'How can I reassure you, Superintendent?'

'You can't. Until I know what this is about.'

'This isn't about your conduct, sir...'

'Oh?'

'A decision was made to suspend Inspector Marshall?'

'Yes… by me.'

'Yes sir. We'd like you to reinstate him, without prejudice, as soon as possible.'

'Oh… why?'

'We believe the Inspector is on the cusp of making a breakthrough in this most important of cases.'

'Making? As he's on suspension, pending reinstatement, he shouldn't be working on anything at all.'

'We feel his reinstatement will advance the case and put us all in a more advantageous position.'

'Do you indeed.'

'If the Inspector is officially returned, a greater share of the credit for resolving this case would naturally accrue to this service, and this station, sir. And reflect well on your leadership.'

'If you think you can flatter or manipulate me like some debutante, you're very much mistaken.'

'Sir, it would be an enormous help to us. We would be extremely grateful. I would even go as far as to say it would guarantee you would be considered for an award by the honours commission.'

'OH?'

'May we look forward to his return tomorrow, Superintendent?'

'I'm not sure if I had time to sign him off yet, officially, what with all my extra duties; perhaps we would all be in agreement that it never happened. Let's just say it was a ruse on my part to get him out of the room to calm down, shall we, and say no more about it?' said the policeman, taking off his hat.

'I've no objections to putting it down as a free and frank exchange of views. Have you, Bruce?'

'Can't say I recall the conversation, sir.'

'Excellent! We'll look forward to his return then.'

'May I ask if you've spoken to Marshall yet?'

'It's our responsibility to interview anyone we believe can help us, Superintendent. That may include Mr Marshall.'

'Of couse, of course, but…'

'Thank you for your time, Superintendent. We will be certain to inform the Home Secretary how helpful you've been, through our own superiors.'

'Yes… of course. Is that all?'

'Thank you, sir.'

D'Ascoyne returned his hat to its proper place and strode out of the office, without ceremony, leaving the two agents feeling like they had just had a very awkward conversation with one or both of their fathers.

'Well, that was – awkward,' commented the younger agent to his superior.

'It's all part of the job – ruffling feathers. The sooner you realise that the easier it becomes. Mr D'Ascoyne is a good sort. I can't say I'm not sympathetic to his predicament, but here we are – between a rock and a hard place. Just remember we've got a job to do, Bruce.'

'Yes, sir.'

'Has anyone come up with an explanation for the explosion in the old town, the one that levelled that nightclub – Mystery City?'

'The fire brigade said it was a gas leak, sir. A cracked inlet pipe in an annexe leaking into the main building. The fire door was wedged open and a gas ring in the kitchen on the other side ignited it.'

'Any casualties?'

'Two males. Interestingly, one of them was that gangster from Aberdeen. The one you told me about on the train from York.'

'Cod War Crosbie! I'll be damned! Did they find his body?'

'They'd be lucky to find anything bigger than a shirt button, let alone a body. Everything that wasn't pulverised or burnt to ashes is just dust, sir. The heat from the fire was so intense it even melted the RSJs in the attic. The fire brigade wouldn't let me on the site. Accident investigators and gas engineers were still making it safe. There's a demolition firm coming to level it tomorrow after the Health and Safety Exec have finished. I didn't want to stick my nose in. As we aren't officially here. The only other official presence they had there was a priest giving some sort of blessing...'

'So Crosbie was in there when it blew, was he?'

'They found a pulverised piece of shoe in his size with some blood on it, sir. On the top of someone's television aerial a couple of streets away. It's the biggest piece of evidence we've got left.'

'Well, Special Branch will be pleased to close the file on that one. They've got better things to do than keep tabs on home-grown psychopaths. There was a friend of his there, too – James Stone.'

'On the premises, sir.'

'Has that been confirmed?'

'We found some scraps of a bedsheet with blood on it.'

'But no body?'

'No sir… but there's nothing bigger than a matchbox left. Everything's been pulverised and burnt to a crisp.'

'So how did the bedsheet survive the fire?'

'It was smeared with PVA, sir. Then covered in brick dust.'

'So – Stone's dead as well. *Good…* that's a bonus. He had the makings of an even worse human being than his boss. They won't be missed.'

Whitborough's guest MI5 agents then spent the rest of the day in their private suite at Whitborough Police Station, conducting monitoring tests of their covert recording equipment, and examining emergency services recording logs from the Easter weekend. What they hadn't prepared for was the frequency of Inspector Marshall's methane discharges, and his snoring. It was going to be hard to argue that their recording log was not actually the record of a human subject, but the audio recording of a dairy herd with severe flatulence – or a family of bears in hibernation. But with their limited resources any editing was out of the question unless there was a drastic escalation in hostilities.

Once he was back inside the comfortable sanctuary of his office suite, D'Ascoyne selected the dialling button for Inspector Marshall's home phone and put the receiver to his ear. It was more than two minutes before he answered.

'Marshall?'

'Oh – hello, sir, I must say this is an unexpected surprise… may I ask why it is that you're calling?'

'We need you back at the station.'

'For a disciplinary hearing, sir, I need at least fourteen days' notice to appoint a representative from the federation, and my legal counsel.'

'Look – forget about that… can you come back tomorrow?'

'Am I to understand that my suspension has been quashed, sir – or just suspended pending further evidence?'

'Look Ray, it was just a, a…'

'Mistake, sir?'

'Yes… it was never a suspension, as such, just an unfortunate choice of words on my part… it was just a ruse to get you out of the interview room to avoid inflaming tensions… in the interests of maintaining…'

'So I've not actually been formally suspended… there's no paperwork filed?'

'Well… not exactly… look… I… can we just forget about all that?'

'So I'm reinstated? No entry of suspension on my personnel record?'

'Look, can we just forget about the whole thing. Like I said, I haven't actually sent off the paperwork yet anyway.'

'Shall we record my enforced departure as a leave of absence, sir, for personal reasons?'

'Yes, yes… I don't see any problem… can I ask if you've… if you've seen anyone from the federation yet… regarding our… er…?'

'No, sir. I haven't seen anyone from the federation. Or my solicitor.'

'Ahh, excellent. May we see you in the morning then?'

'I'm afraid I've got an appointment tomorrow, sir. What about the day after?'

'The day after… of course. Of course, I trust you're well… no health issues?'

'None, sir, in spite of the fags. And the cigars.'

'Well, don't over-do it, Ray.'

'Moderation in everything, sir. Just one little problem, sir…'

'Oh?'

'I'll need someone to push me around if George isn't up to it.'

'What do you mean?'

'I'm temporarily off my feet, you might say. Both ankles in plaster. The explosion on Rope Walk.'

'YOU WERE ON ROPE WALK?'

'No, sir. Taking a stroll in St Mary's churchyard. Copped a couple of record decks on the ankles.'

'**Copped what?**' What do you mean **copped**?'

'**Struck,** sir. As in – hit by.'

'Are you all right, Marshall?'

'Apart from two broken ankles, I'm fit as a buck rat, sir.'

'Don't be facetious.'

'No, sir. How is Sergeant Broadhead, sir?'

'He's fine. Look – I'll have a word with personnel. I'm sure we can get you in somehow, even in a wheelchair. God knows we need an experienced head around here at the moment. I can't work miracles with a depleted team…'

'Very kind of you to say so, sir. I'm looking forward to getting back.'

'Sergeant Broadhead has been very industrious these last few days. Do you have a video cassette from R&E at your home address? The sergeant signed out the original here.'

'The tape of the ghost in the lobby? I don't suppose you've seen it, sir?'

'I did catch a little of the footage, when I was calling on Broadhead,' he said, uncomfortably. 'But I wouldn't like to give an opinion on it. We certainly can't make assumptions until it's been properly analysed.'

'Barry's already checked it over, sir. Nothing wrong with it.'

'Sergeant Whitefield's examined it? Is he qualified to do that?'

'Used to run a film processing lab, sir. Should know his stuff.'

'So it's genuine? What about atmospherics... couldn't that account for it?'

'If it was atmospherics, sir, it would have affected the whole negative, not just the top corner.'

'Oh...'

'Are there just two copies of it?'

'Unless Sergeant Whitefield's made another, sir.'

'Nothing else appeared in reception with the er... the er...'

'Apparition, sir?'

'Let's not jump to conclusions.'

'Anything else, sir?'

'Physical evidence?'

'Such as...'

'A document folder...'

'Nothing I'm aware of, sir.'

'Moyne seemed to think Elland found a folder in reception after the er... the...'

'Thing, sir?'

'Yes. But there's no receipt stub, or a document retainer record. Now Moyne and Elland are denying there was ever such a folder.'

'Difficult for me to comment, sir, in my absence...' replied Marshall pointedly. 'All this death and destruction is going to have an effect on all of us I think, sir. It's definitely made its mark on me. Thank God I've got a bathroom downstairs.'

'It will help us all when we make some progress that can't be claimed by outside agencies,' lamented D'Ascoyne. 'I'm counting on you to come up with a lead, Ray.'

'Yes, sir. I'll do my best – as ever.'

'I'm counting on you, Marshall. Don't let me down. Just out of interest, how long are you going to be in this wheelchair?'

'Six weeks.'

Once he had had some time to think, Marshall rang his sergeant at home and discussed his plans for his return, beginning with a series of interviews and cross-checking facts and statements, then follow-up interviews and visits to new witnesses.

'We'll start off by questioning the junior staff at the Shirestones, then move up the food chain, George.'

'What about Beautimann?'

'He's as guilty as hell. And he knows we know. But we've got to find the evidence.'

'Of whatever he's guilty of?'

'Mmmm. I want you to send one of our DCs into town to sniff around the record stores, and the rock and punk pubs. See if we can find the owner of that coloured hair that forensics found beside the pampas grass at Carr Wold Parkway. When you've arranged that we'll go and see old Chipping at the Museum, and step on his Hush Puppies to see if we can make him squeal.'

Chapter Twenty-Five

Saturday Night's All Right for Fighting.

On Saturday evening the best-dressed senior ladies of the Black Hand Coven – Violet Penrose, Maureen Moment and Joy Blanchard – and a semi-detached Phyllis Elliott sashayed into the wood-panelled function room at the rear of the Jack of Both Sides, from the old flagstones of Passions Place, saw that their favourite seats were vacant, then tottered triumphantly towards the corner booth and dropped into the deeply cushioned seats.

'Mine's a rum and Coke, Mo,' said Violet. 'Make sure Sam don't put any ice in it, it sets me teeth off. What d'you want, Joy?'

'I'll have a Jack and Coke, Mo. No ice in mine either, girl.'

'Phyll?'

'I'll have a Cognac – straight.'

'Do you want ice in yours, love?'

'I'm not fussy, I'll drink it as it comes.'

'Okay. I think I'm going to have a G&T.'

'Mo?'

'Yes, Phyll?'

'Make mine a double.'

As soon as she had extracted herself from her snug, black

Jaeger blouson, Maureen tugged her matching skirt straight and then stood up again, as gracefully as the constraining seams and stretch panels of her undergarments would allow, to check the other booths for anyone who looked like a clergyman or a policeman, returning to their table for her purse before she went to the bar as her sister witches started to rummage inside their bags, slamming all kinds of peculiar implements and small tins essential to the maintenance of womankind onto the table. Joy passed her deck of Tarot cards to Violet to shuffle while she checked her lipstick, and applied more blusher. None of the ladies at the table spoke, as they busied themselves with eyebrow pencils, tweezers and lipsticks, until every blemish and flaw was obliterated.

'It's always so dim in here,' griped Phyllis to the reflection in her compact as they packed away their combs and cosmetics.

'That's the way we like it – ain't it? Gives us a fighting chance against the young 'uns,' muttered Violet – whose deepest desire was to re-visit her misspent youth all over again in a younger body.

Maureen's willingness to stand the first round had less to do with straightforward generosity than a desire to escape the awkward atmosphere between her companions. Going to the serving hatch first was the best excuse she could think of to get herself away from the stillborn punch-up which would undoubtedly come to a head at some point before the night was over. Her act of generosity also necessitated a long stop to count her change under a light bulb that barely illuminated the bottom of her purse; smothered, as it was, by a lampshade that dimmed its light output to the level of a vaguely luminous deep-sea jellyfish dragging its grimy cobwebs through the shadows of the snug on three dirt-encrusted chains.

Apart from the essential apparatus of a twentieth century bar, gas central heating and a Victorian WC with a shrieking cistern, the interior of the Jack of Both Sides had hardly changed in over four hundred years. One of the oldest free houses in Whitborough, and one of the few sources of illumination at the crossroads of Archers Gate and Vexing View, the "fighting" Jack was a model Tudor ale house, with an intrinsically seafaring flavour; as a consequence of having been built by men who were normally employed as shipwrights and carpenters in the port.

Its prettiest aspect displayed a triple jettied fascia overlooking Press Gang Place, beautified with decorative pargeted mouldings. On each of its flanks there was a third-floor flying master bedroom with swing-barrel corners, two saddleback Flemish brick chimney stacks bookending the middle roof, a rope and pulley ale barrel lift in the cellar, at least five ghosts of both sexes, and a poltergeist that threw beer mats and peanuts at the landlord's cat and left puddles of water in embarrassing places.

Within the great black ribcage of its oak beams the nautical themes continued: there were ship's lanterns by the dozen which had been converted to electric lamps wired optimistically into an Italian standard consumer unit; provisions barrels employed as tables; chairs fashioned from hatch covers and spindles sawn from the salvaged poop deck of the wrecked frigate the *Toby Ventriss;* reclaimed masts – mortised and planed for support timbers; deck plank by the hundredweight, and rope gulley collars galore.

The Jack's rear annexe – the favourite haunt of the Black Hand Coven – was affectionately known as the Cannonball Snug on account of its resemblance to the gun deck of an

Elizabethan warship. It had once been the largest partition in the old pub's former stable block; but more than a century after it had ceased to be part of the stables the annexe still had only one window – a stout but rather crude affair from the heyday of the adze with four distorted panes of "pauper's glass" – that the Victorian Society had petitioned to save for posterity.

Scruffy, spartan and lacking any significant natural light, the snug was nevertheless very popular with those few patrons who looked forward to a quiet drink in the privacy of its dark and gloomy closets. At its fireplace end a garland of mooring rope framed a small half-door-cum-serving-hatch in the rear wall from which the occupants could order more drinks; underneath a hovering junkyard of copper pans, kettles, watering cans, typewriters and rusting sabres fastened by hooks and brackets to the ceiling boards. There was also a gallery of portraits depicting the faded faces of long-deceased townsfolk, interrupted here and there by an occasional Van Gogh or Monet nailed to the beams. Though Phyllis, Joy and Violet – the first of the damned to cast their forensic glares upon the furniture beneath the metalwork jungle – weren't entirely certain where the sepia tints ended and the accumulating layers of nicotine and grime began.

'*Have y'seen the state of this rug?*' said Joy, making a face.

'I know, pet,' sighed Violet. 'I'm trying me best not to look at it. Thank God the benches are vinyl; at least they can wipe *them* down. Maureen's ex, Rodney, used to come in here when he was alive. It's the same rug they had back then; the only thing holding it together is the muck.'

'Watch me coat, girls. Oive jus' gotta go change me tights and dab on some *oleum magicale*,' added Joy, over-egging a wink. 'I'll do yoos a spread when oive fixed me legs.'

'*OOOOH you dirty cow…*' howled Violet, slapping the table-top with mock delight.

'Not me legs! The Tarot – you daft mare!' grinned Joy, poking Violet in the ribs with her elbow.

Phyllis – still simmering from one of Violet's jibes – ignored their cackles and returned her attention to her finger nails, frowning at her cuticles with studied disdain and passing a dagger-like nail file over some imaginary imperfections to give herself something to do; before she made a half-hearted effort to rejoin the conversation.

'Didn't Maureen's Rodney get killed in the paper?'

'*No – he got blown up in France,*' replied Violet, sarcastically.

'Oh – sorry I spoke,' said Phyllis sniffily. 'I'll keep me trap shut next time, shall I?'

Violet pretended to miss her near neighbour's little dig, then continued her diatribe on the state of the floor. 'It's more bloody shitminster that Axminster – this rug,' she continued, looking to Joy, as she slowly inched out between their bench and table. 'If it were any dirtier you could grow bloody potatoes on it. You'd think they'd get a new one down since the price of the bloody drinks went through the roof. If any of our lot come in – don't let 'em put me bag on the floor. I'll never get the bloody stains out. Are we moving on after the rest of 'em get 'ere?'

'I think Aleister said there was some kind of tribute act at the Dickens tonight,' answered Maureen, from the serving hatch nearby.

'What… like a caberett?' smirked Violet, mispronouncing her French with glee.

'There's a comedian too.'

'A singer an' a comedian?'

145

'That's what he said.'

'Two for one then… Are we going out for summat to eat after?'

'I could murder a Chinese. I'm flippin' ravenous,' complained Phyllis, louder than was really necessary, as Joy and Violet tried their very best not to register her presence.

'We'll have to ask Derek. I don't know for certain what we're doing after the Dick,' said Maureen. 'Where do you go when you eat out, Vi?'

'Me and Kieran usually go to Luchinelli's. They do this bruschetta starter, well – you've never tasted anything like it…' she cooed, closing her eyes and puckering her lips. 'Bloody fantastic… their pizzas are reet tasty too. Not like them limp ones you get in Venice Pizza and Napoleos.'

'Napoli's?'

'Aye – them an' all…' she said haughtily, annoyed at being corrected mid-flow. 'Luchinelli's put capers an' arty-chocks on their pizzas – that's class, that is. I wish our Kieran were more adventurous with his grub, though. He still orders the same bloody thing – *every time*. If they ran out of bloody pepperoni sausage or ham, God only knows what we'd do. We'd probably have to go home. But when we're really flush we go to Bertuccio's. I swear to God, their monkfish pasta parcels – sex on a fork…' she cackled.

Maureen blanched. Then hastily changed the subject. 'What's a caper?'

'They're like them petit pois'es – in brine. Like wrinkled fairies' bollocks,' said Violet with a completely straight face – taking a huge swig of rum and Coke.

'Oh… I don't know whether I'd like something like that,' said Maureen, grimacing, 'they sound a bit sharp.'

Phyllis lit a replacement cigarette and blew a resentful cloud of smoke between her companions, who tried their best not to notice.

'They sell them capers in Costcutter, Mo,' added Violet, 'you can buy capers anywhere nowadays. I don't suppose you like curry either then – do you?'

'Curry? No. Spicy food doesn't agree with me, pet... I get heartburn if I even look at an onion. Or when someone blows smoke in my face...' she said caustically. 'I'm not a great lover of foreign food. My idea of heaven is a recliner, a Black Forest gateau and a double dose of *Corrie*. If Bert's not tried to hump my leg then I let him lick me box out.'

Phyllis's mouth fell open and her cigarette dropped into the open mouth of her handbag; although she didn't appear to have noticed it was no longer glued to her lipstick.

'*You what!*' cried Violet.

'I let him have my cake boxes. He licks them clean, then rips them up.'

'*OH... RIGHT...*'

'Are you all right, Vi?' asked Maureen, suddenly aware her friend had gone rather pale.

'Oh aye... I'm fine... *I'm fine* – now *I've got you right*,' she muttered, eyes still wide with shock. 'I think I need another Bacardi,' she muttered, eyelashes flaring... 'Did you want one, pet?'

'Thanks Vi, but I'll skip this one I think, I'm a bit delicate tonight.'

'You don't say... I feel a bit strange meself... all of a sudden...' said Violet, still trying to block a mental image of Maureen and Bert enjoying unnatural practices.

'I've got a bit of indigestion, I think,' muttered Maureen.

147

'That's a shame,' mumbled Phyllis under her breath.

'Can you smell something burning, girls?' asked Maureen suddenly, looking around the room.

'Are you two going to ignore me all night – just because I lost your bloody cat?' snapped Phyllis.

'You're on fire, Phyll,' said Violet, giving a nod to the small blaze that had just caught in the depths of her companion's handbag.

'OH FRIGGING 'ELL!' cried Phyllis, upending her Cognac into the flames.

'*Shut the top of your purse, you daft cow! It'll snuff it out!*' yelled Violet, panicking, as a blue and pink fireball, borne from the slosh of their companion's double brandy, burst from the top of the handbag.

'*Don't call me a daft cow!*' barked Phyllis.

'PUT IT OUT!' squealed Maureen.

The landlord, Samuel Glasscock, poked his head through the serving hatch to try and locate the source of the scent of the burning leather and brandy, saw Violet staring back at him with a rolled up newspaper, then ducked back inside the safety of the main bar.

'They shouldn't be too much longer, the others,' said Maureen, trying to deflect from the furious beating that Violet was doling out on the scorched leather handbag belonging to her colleague.

'It's out now – okay!' snorted Phyllis.

'Well – that were exciting... d'you know Mo... I can't remember the last time we had a night out. It must have been the night before we brought Deirdre Cousins to darkness,' said Violet after getting her breath back.

Phyllis slammed her purse on the table, making Maureen

and Violet twitch, then stormed off to the toilet with her smoking bag.

'Good riddance…' grumbled Vi. 'Making us jump,' she muttered resentfully.

'Are we being a bit harsh on her?' asked Maureen guiltily.

'*Harsh? Harsh…?* – She lost me f★★king cat – Maureen!'

'Oh come on, Vi – the cat ran off by itself.'

'Only cos she let go of it…'

'Oh for goodness sake!'

'I'm not letting her off, Maureen. Our Brinsley still hasn't come back.'

'Well, I'm not surprised – after getting soaked in spit, pus an' snake venom. I wouldn't go rushing back to somebody who put me through that, either. But it's hardly Phyllis's fault, she got covered in it too. Like the rest of us. I had to take a day off work until my bloody rash cleared up; my hands looked like they'd been dipped in Ribena.'

The witches sat in silence for a few minutes, letting their tempers cool, then resumed their conversation as if nothing had happened.

'Our old pal joined the Rosicrucians, you know,' said Maureen.

'*Who… Phyllis?*'

'*No not Phyll – Deidre…* Poor old Dee…' sighed Maureen.

'She's not that old, she's only forty-two, Mo.'

'Is she? What on earth does she put on her face…? Anyway – she probably feels a bit safer with *that lot* at the Lodge. At least they don't go swinging cockerels around their heads on a washing line cord. I'll never be able to look at a chicken's beak again without breaking into a sweat… I wonder if they managed to stitch her ear back on…' pondered

149

Maureen, suppressing a shudder, as she remembered the unintentionally grisly climax of one of their more fraught initiations. 'We've not exactly been blessed with luck just recently, have we... the devil looks after his own – my arse,' she muttered.

'So is Derek definitely coming along tonight?'

'I should hope so... he said he'd meet us later in the Dickens. Elsie at Valhalla said she might pop out for an hour – if she can get Mark out from under his bloody motorbikes to watch the bar.'

'He's not as daft as he looks is he – your Derek? He must have seen the state of this place.'

'Derek's not daft, Vi,' said Maureen icily, scolding her companion. 'He's not *my* anything, anyway.'

'Bit of a fox in his day... wouldn't you say, Mo?'

'We work together – that's all.'

'OH HELL! The men just walked past the window,' said Violet, panicking. 'They've brought that perv from Beehive Taxis; sit next to me on the bench will you, Mo, so that dirty twat Jamie can't put his paws on me knees.'

'Charming...'

Madame 'Joy' Blavatsky suddenly emerged from the toilet in fresh tights, checked her décolletage, straightened her blouse and stared at the two untouched drinks beside her coat; at the same time Phyllis returned to their bench with another vodka. 'Are *both* o' those moine, girls?'

'Aye lass. Mo got us two each. Get yer arse on the bench quick, Joy, Cosmo's outside,' snapped Violet.

'Is there enough room for lil' old me on there?'

'We'll make room... I'm not having that dirty bastard thinking he can squeeze in next to me.'

'Pass me yer bag, me lover – oi'll stow it under our table.'

'I'll keep mine on me lap thanks, Joy, the floors in 'ere are f**king filthy.'

'Put 'em on the chair then, Vi,' said Maureen.

'Good thinking, girl.'

'Are my tights straight?'

'You've still got it, Joy.'

'Thanks girls – hush now, the men are coming in. Let's tease the buggers, cross yer legs, girls, and flash the lippy. Come on Phyll – get sat down,' said Joy grudgingly. 'Has something been burning in here?'

'Speaking to me now, are you?' snapped Phyllis – looming over their bench with a fresh apple brandy.

'I haven't forgotten about my cat,' muttered Violet.

'Get off your high horse, Vi, I can no more hold onto a cat that wants to bolt when it's covered in goo, than you can hold onto a bloody husband,' countered Phyllis, plonking herself down at the end of their bench.

Before Violet could come back with a cutting reply, the outside door to the snug creaked open, for the second time, as the four male members of the coven peeped into the gloomy interior.

'Hello girls – room for a small one?' chuckled Jamie Osbourne, the owner of Beehive Taxis, winking at the four women squeezed together on their bench.

'We'll have another round, ta,' said Violet, smirking tautly.

'Hiya Jamie,' beamed Phyllis, 'you can have my seat, pet. *I'm* off to powder me nose. The girls aren't talking to me.'

Violet's brittle smile dropped off her face like a horseshoe knocked off its nail.

'Hello my lovelies! *Fabulously* turned out as usual – are you all right for drinks?' enquired Ronald, rushing in behind his friend Jamie in a pretend fluster.

'Thanks, Ron – Jamie's getting us a refill. Sit down next to Joy, pet, and tell us what you've been up to,' said Maureen craftily.

'So where am I going to sit?' moaned the coven's own "Thrice Great Hermes".

'When you've got us all a drink we'll move us coats an' yer can sit down on one o' them stools in front,' said Violet. 'So we can keep an eye on yer wandering 'ands.'

'Just move me bolero jacket, Brett darlin' – an' get your cute liddle bum on that stool,' said Joy, directing their youngest male member to a vacant spot beside the short side of their table.

'Thanks, Mrs Turner,' said Brett, blushing furiously.

'Make sure Jamie gets you a drink too, lover,' said Joy lasciviously.

'Put t'wood back in t'hole, Ron,' said Vi. 'While Cosmo's at the bar.'

'What's that, Vi?'

'Shut the door – me ankles feel like f★★king ice in that draft.'

Roy Rudd, Whitborough's answer to the famous Occutist Aleister Crowley, suddenly appeared from the main bar, pricked his thumb with an iron pin and smeared the blood on the top of a chair nearby that took his fancy. 'Right, that's me set,' he said.

'Don't you try and sit near us, ya bastard – we don't sup with cat murderers,' said Violet.

Maureen looked heavenwards and sighed reproachfully.

'I haven't actually murdered any cats yet, Violet,' replied Roy, trying hard not to sound confrontational.

'Don't give me any of that crap – you were dead set on carving up that poor puss last weekend with that bloody great Bowie knife of yours.'

'Violet – put a sock in it, love…' groaned Ronnie. 'We're supposed to be chums together having a friendly night out.'

'CHUMS MY ARSE!'

'I wouldn't say that too loudly in the Dickens,' said Phyllis. 'We'll get marked down as rough trade.'

'Is your Tony coming out, Ron?' asked Maureen, attempting to restore some politeness to the conversation.

★

In the Beautimann household, Derek forced himself to change clothes – swapping his grey Prince of Wales suit and black brogues for a navy yachting blazer, stone chinos and blue loafers – whilst he fretted over the prospect of another drink-soaked evening in town with his recalcitrant fellow Satanists. With such a lot on his mind it was going to be an awkward couple of hours. Unfortunately, it was now too late for him to bow out without damaging his fraying credibility. He realised he was going to have to show his face and then try to think of a good enough reason to excuse himself, once he had said his piece; before his colleagues inevitably disgraced themselves.

★

'So, I hear you gave the vet at Aveyou Nympton the finger, Maureen,' said Jamie, returning from the serving hatch with a tray full of glasses.

'What!' she asked, horrified. *'How do you know?'*

'I heard all about it from the man himself. It were me that took the poor sod home from the hospital, love. I'd get yourself a good solicitor, if I were you.'

'What's all this about then?' said Joy.

'Spill the beans, Mo…' said Vi.

'Bert bit Mr Reynard at the vets in Aveyou Nympton. Took his blummin' finger off,' said Maureen sheepishly.

'YOU'RE KIDDING!'

'I'd hate to see *that* bill,' muttered Ron

'I know he's always been one of those dogs that wants to have it away with your ankle, but I didn't realise he was snappy too,' said Roy.

'Snappy is putting it a bit mildly. You might as well use the same adjective for a crocodile,' muttered Phyllis.

'What's an adjective?' hissed Violet into Joy's ear.

'You should know that frum school, Vi.'

'What – domestic science?'

'No – English… you daft sod.'

'Well it can't be that important. I've bin managing without it for years, ain't I?'

'It's a *them*, not… oh never mind…' sighed Joy, leering at Brett.

'So what did they do with Mr Reynard's digit, Maureen – did they stitch it back on?'

'Oh no, he jumped right out the examination room window – I haven't seen the little bastard since.'

'Oh heck!'

'Will he come back?'

'Oh yes – eventually; the little sod's probably halfway to bloody Seamer by now, but he's got all his tags on. He'll be in somebody's garden before too long, after he's rolled in something dead, and sired a few more little bastards. It's not the first time he's run off, and it won't be the last. I've been on first name terms with Reggie at the dog pound since I got Bert.'

'What would he want to go to Seamer for?'

'There's a butcher's there that sells chittlings.'

'Chittlings?'

'Guts. Offal – boiled and bleached. The little bugger goes mad for it.'

'I think I'm going to be sick,' groaned Brett.

'You're a sensitive lad, *I like that*,' beamed Joy, flashing a megawatt smile in the direction of her prey.

Violet coughed and gave her friend Ronald a withering stare.

'Ronnie?'

'Yes, Vi?'

'Get your hand off me leg.'

'Sorry Vi, I didn't realise I was…'

'Next time – I'll stub me fag out on it.'

'So – are we waiting for anybody? I don't know about you lot but I'm starving!' said Phyllis, pulling on her coat.

'Are we going out to eat before the Dickens, girls?' asked Ron sheepishly.

'Nobody said anything to me about going to a restaurant…' said Jamie. 'I thought we were just going for a few drinks. Has someone booked a table somewhere?'

'Not as far as I know, Jamie,' said Maureen. 'Derek never suggested anything, he just said he'd meet us after nine o'clock in the Dickens for drinks and a chat.'

'I suppose it's up to us then,' said Jamie.

'I'm not hungry,' said Vi. 'I doubt Maureen wants to go out to eat with a vet's bill like she's got.'

'Violet!'

'Sorry pet… I'm just saying…'

'I can speak for myself – thank you. I'm not as *impoverished* as some of you think. In fact I've just paid to go to South Africa. On a cruise.'

'Oh I just *LOVE* cruise ships,' cooed Jamie.

'Who's looking after Bert for you, Mo – presuming he comes back?'

'I've booked him in kennels.'

'Oim just sticking to the pubs tonight. Can't afford to eat out mid-week,' said Joy sourly, siding with Violet.

'Well you can do what you like, I'm off to Lings. I'll meet the rest of you in the Dickens,' said Phyllis. 'Are you coming, Jamie?'

'Thanks, Phyll, but I'll stick to liquids tonight, luv.'

'Please yourself.'

'Can I come?' said Brett. 'I had nothing to eat all day.'

'Of course you can, love. If you don't mind being seen with an older woman.'

Joy's half-empty glass of Bacardi and lime crashed down onto the table.

'Roy?'

'Yes Vi?'

'Drink up. You're coming down town with us.'

'She did that on purpose… did you see what she's done?' hissed Joy as she watched Brett open the door for Phyllis.

'Where are we going next?' asked Maureen grimly, trying to change the subject again.

156

'The Centurion,' said Violet, grinning.

'Living dangerously tonight, aren't we, Vi?' said Joy, still smarting from the loss of another potential conquest.

'Shields up!' quipped Ronnie, crossing himself. 'I'll be in the corner booth, after I've checked it for bloodstains.'

'They've just had a refit,' said Vi, indignantly. 'It's a lovely pub.'

'Oh aye. It's a lovely pub. It's just the bloody punters that you need to watch,' said Joy. 'Give us me cards, Vi – might as well put 'em away now. Don't look as though anyone wants to get their fortune told now, do it?'

'Are we going to the Dick straight after?' asked Roy sheepishly.' They won't let me in the Centurion.'

'It's their opening night, pet, just keep yer head down and you'll be fine. Is everyone ready then? Let's make a move.'

'So what's the real reason Derek's coming out with us commoners, Mo? Has he got something to tell us?' asked Vi, as the party walked slowly up towards Whitborough town centre along the quiet winding streets of the old town.

'Does he have to have a reason?'

'Well, when does he ever come out with us? Unless it's to break bad news or to try and sell one of us a shit sandwich.'

'Do you have to be so coarse, Vi?'

'I'm being blunt. If people don't like it they can bugger off.' Violet took a few seconds to collect her thoughts then continued with her line of enquiry. 'You two might work in a law firm but you can't pull the wool over my eyes – so what's the big announcement? Is he going to join the Golden Dawn?'

'It's not my place to say.'

'Me an' Joy got an announcement of our own anyway, Mo.'

157

'Oh?'

'We're setting up an introduction agency between the two of us. For people who like alternative lifestyles an' that. Wanted to ask if you'd lend us a few quid to start up now you gots your money from Rodney's life insurance? We'll pay you back o' course.'

'An introduction agency?'

'Aye. There's nothing for women like us except the bloody personals in *Prediction*. Or the *Glastonbury Herald*. We're a bit too "pagan" for Dateline – and there's only so many ads you can put in before you have to call it a day. No real men for us. Just a load of washed-up old farts with greasy hair driving tatty cars covered in CAMRA stickers. So we thought we'd do something about it before we turn into bloody nuns.'

'What are you going to call it – Jump-a-witch?' crowed Jamie.

'Mind your own, Cosmo.'

'Always a pleasure, Violet.'

'Vi to you…'

'It sounds quite exciting, Vi – if you need an old queen's perspective, you let me know, dearie.'

'Thanks, Ron.'

'Have you got a name, girls?'

'The Wicked Tree Introduction Agency,' said Violet proudly. 'We're 'aving business cards done. And lettered 'eads. Posters for Glastonbury. An' the Druids' solstice bash.'

'An' the Green Man Fair at Okehampton,' added Joy.

'Mmmm, very classy.'

Meanwhile, at the witches' night out, Tony "Lee" Presley Cheung made his entrance over the chorus of the Doors' "Break on Through", between the twin pillars of the Seabrook crisps order and six boxes of Monster Munch that were stacked at the end of the Dickens Hotel's Fagin Bar. A five foot one, leather-clad miniature of cool in aviator sunglasses and cuban heels. Dressed in a three-quarter length black velvet frock coat, with black satin lapels, black trousers and shirt, Tony "Lee" Cheung came forth like a conquering hero, holding up a black cane with a huge silver pommel in the shape of a snarling panther's head, towing a Mothercare baby truck piled with sequin-trimmed red towels with a pair of black lace knickers tied to the handle.

'You've gort tae be fecken jo-kenn…' said Isla Binnie.

'Oh – my – God.'

'This is a joke… *right?*'

Tony's wife, Gloria, killed the main lights in the bar and switched on the overhead spotlight into which her husband strode, karate chopping the air in front of his microphone. A chilly silence enveloped the audience and then the lights came back on, as Tony launched into "Heartbreak Hotel".

'WELL SINCE MY BAYBEE REFT ME – AN FOUND NEW PLACE TO DWELL,

DOWN END, OF RONE-REE SHREET – HEARTBREAK HOTEL…

I BEE SHRO RONE-REE BAYBEE

I BEE SHRO RONE-REE

I BEE SHRO RONE-REE – I COULD FRY.

'THO' IS ALWAYS CWOWDED,

IT STILL GOT VACANT WOOM,

FOR BWOKEN HEARTED LOVER TO RUN AROUND WITH BWOOM,

I BEE SHRO RONE-REE BAYBEE
I BEE SHRO RONE-REE
I BEE SHRO RONE-REE – I COULD FRY

'WELL BELL HOP TEAR KEEP FWOWING
AN' DESK CWERK – HE GOT SACK.'

'Is this performance meant to be a parody…?' enquired Derek, rooted to the spot in horror and awe.

'Parody…? It's the bravest piss-take I've ever seen, man.'

'He's *atrocious… Absolutely atrocious…*'

'Well enjoy it, Dez. Short-arse Presley only does a forty-minute set before he needs a peanut satay 'n' jelly spring roll.'

'I don't think I've ever *enjoyed* anything less. He's murdering the legacy of the greatest popular entertainer of the twentieth century!'

'You haven't got enough drink inside you, Dezzie, that's your trouble. This twonk is a friggin genius, he just doesn't know it.'

'I understand we're having an informal get together, but my name is Derek. So would you please not call me *Dez. Or that other name…*'

'Sorry, boss… Mine's a pint o' Stella, by the way – *when you're ready.*'

'Oh… are we…'

'It's your round, Mr B.'

'But…'

'Joy an' Violet are on rum 'n' Coke, Isla's 'aving straight double vodka – her toe's still giving her some gyp. Phyll's on vodka – straight, Colin's a Guinness, Harry Germain's on G&T, Crowley's is a Jack 'n' Coke and your mate sour face is drinking white wine and soda,' said Thrice Great Hermes, cocking his head at Maureen who was just coming out of the ladies'. 'The rest of us are on John Smiths. Except Casanova. He's driving Joan of Arc back to 'er Mum's.'

'But I thought we were all buying our own drinks?'

'Buying our own drinks? I don't think that'd go down too well… you'll kill the team spirit stone dead, saying stuff like that.'

'But I can't possibly drink as much as the rest of you. I'm just not used to it.'

'Don't *fret,* Derek. Just relax. If you can't finish your drink then leave it.'

'Look, I'm prepared to chip in, but I can't drink every drink that's bought for me. I'll have to leave most of them. You'll be wasting your money.'

'So? We'll waste our money – it's our money to waste.'

'I'll finish you off, Mister Beautimann,' said Brett earnestly.

Ronnie Gould, the camp Comte de St Germain, almost choked on his drink.

'Don't worry love, I'll carry you 'ome,' said Mary, putting her hand on Derek's knee.'

'That won't be necessary, Mary… Will you please remove your hand from my leg? Thank you.'

'Only being friendly…'

'I don't wish to be rude, Mary, but it's not appropriate or welcome.'

'Suit yourself…'

'Derek's a *gentleman,* Mary. An' 'ee's married. Eees not common – loike you,' said Alice.

'You cheeky COW! You're not even a *proper* witch…'

'SSSHHHHHH!'

'Mary – will you keep your gob shut – *do you want the whole bloody world to know our business?*' said Maureen. 'Can I have a word with you, Derek?' she added.

'Yes – of course,' said Derek, grateful for the intervention. 'Let's go into the lobby, shall we… outside?' he suggested.

'That was timely.'

'I knew this was a bad idea. Any time after opening time is a bad time with this lot. I told you that you needed to see them before the pubs open. I'm going to make my excuses and go home soon before they start fighting amongst each other. Did you ever go back to the plateau?' asked Maureen quietly, as they left the function room and walked slowly into the lobby looking for a quiet corner.

'No – and I don't intend to either until all this business settles down. The bag should be safe enough where it is for now…'

'What did that policeman want?' asked Maureen, returning to the subject of Inspector Marshall and Detective Sergeant Broadhead's visit to their office a few days before. 'He knows something, doesn't he?'

'He's just fishing, Maureen. He knows *I'm involved*, but he hasn't got a case. He must have a source – but they're either unreliable or underage for a criminal case. Or it's someone in the coven making mischief.'

'Underage? But who's under…'

'Humpty Dumpty.'

'Oh Lord – I'd forgotten about that lad… surely he wouldn't have been able to see any of us clearly inside that great lumpy head. What happened to him anyway?'

'Humpty Dumpty had a great fall… off the cliff.'

'OH!'

'Don't worry – he was inside a great big papier mache safety cell. And it's not a very big cliff, is it?' said Derek, unconcerned.

'The poor little imp! You don't think it could be Alan Chipping?'

'Alan? Absolutely not. He doesn't know anything about the coven. He's as keen to stay out of court as I am. No, it's not Alan.'

'What about that escaped lunatic that ruined our circle?'

'I've no idea who that was, Maureen – but one thing I am sure of – he wasn't on the right side of the law.'

'God – what a mess.'

'You haven't said anything to Isla Binnie, have you? About Tony?'

'No, I haven't.'

'Good. Then we won't go over that again.'

'What do you think that thing was – that looked like a wolf… could it have come through with Tetarzepamdomes?'

'It was probably a minor demon of some kind.'

'Minor! It was huge!'

'I don't want to think about that now. We've got more pressing concerns.'

'We certainly have. Violet and Joy are drunk as sailors. Has she asked to borrow your *De Occulta Philosophia?*'

'No. But she's going to have to promise me she won't read any of my papers again while she's eating, if she wants to borrow anything at all in future. She ruined my collectors' copy of the *Golden Dawn Rituals*. There was pesto on the jacket, curry sauce on the chapter page and brown sauce all over the index. It looks more like the menu from a school canteen than a precious manuscript.'

'WELL I, GORRA RORRA RIVVING TO DO,
WHOLE RORRA ROVVING TO DO,
COME ON BAY-BEE, TOO MAKE IT FUN,
IT TAKE TWO
OH YES – I, GORRA RORRA RIVVING TO
DO – HOE RORRA ROVVIN TO DO
NO ONE WHO I RAVVER DO IT WIV RAN
YOU.

'WELL YOU PRETTIEST GIRL I SEEN,
BUT YOU TREAT, SO DAMN MEAN,
SEE WAY YOU ACT – IS WAY BEYOND
DESPAIR, UH – HUH,
…WELL, TIME IS WASTING,
I AIN'T GOING DOWN YOUR BUS
STATION
AIN'T KNOW 'BOUT YOU, I GONNA GET
MY SHARE…'

By the end of his third song Tony had won over almost all of his detractors; the jeers and howls of laughter had turned to cheers, whistles and giggles, and waves of applause broke out as he went down onto one knee and cradled his microphone between short fat fingers – pressed flat in a gesture of prayer for his peerless rendition of "In the ghetto".

'Get 'em off!' yelled Violet, swaying gently on her stool.

'Don't serve that woman anything alcoholic, Jordan. And keep an eye on the rest of them,' said Simon, the bar manager, leaning into the ear of one of his bar staff.

'Calm down, Vi, the bar staff are giving you the look,' said Ron.

'Giving *me* the look – *I'll curse the bloody lot of 'em!*'

'*Shuuush!*'

'*Oh sod 'em! Basssssterds…*'

'Come on, Vi – we're gwane outsoide for a while,' said Joy, holding her friend upright at the elbow.

'But Elvishishon…'

'Elvis is dead, Vi. He doid on the toilet, an' if you have another rum an' Coke, maid, you'll be dead on yer arse too. Oime gonna get you a glass of water an' you can sit out in the fresh air with me until you sober up.'

'Where's Phyll gone?'

'She's probably still in Lings with Brett.'

'*Cow.*'

'I arranged this on the pretext that we were having a few quiet drinks. Not a bawdy pub crawl!'

'You should know Joy, Violet, Jamie and the rest of our lot are fond of a drink. You've got to catch them early – before they get too merry.'

'Yes, I can see that.'

'Which means we'll have to have *another* meeting. They're not going to remember anything you say to them now, you might as well go home after me if you're not going to get into the spirit of things.'

'I have every intention of doing just that,' said Derek, before his attention was drawn back to the stage. 'My memory of Elvis Presley's Las Vegas period is a little sketchy, Maureen, but I'm fairly sure there weren't any trombone players or bongo drums in the TCB band,' added Derek.

'I'll be back in a tick, I've just got to go and powder my nose.'

Inside the disused attic water tanks of the Dickens Hotel,

165

the demon seed of Tetarzepamdomestoz had toiled night and day to re-constitute itself from the mildly toxic but plentiful remains of dead mice, woodlice and bird droppings in its temporary home. It was also fortunate in having some particularly virulent samples of legionnaires' disease bacteria, from the rust- and limescale-tainted puddles at the bottom of the old Victorian header tanks, from which to re-build its essence before it was strong enough again to hunt.

An unexpected bonus had arrived in its domain soon after dawn – on the day of Tony Cheung's concert – in the form of a sick herring gull; the victim of a spoiled tray of curry and chips. The bird had entered the roof space through the gap left by a fallen soffit board, and expired on a crossbeam from the effects of ingesting a curry sauce that had been accidentally supercharged with double the recommended measure of curry powder mixed with some sump-fresh marine diesel. It was scooped up and absorbed before it was cold.

The demonic nemesis of the Black Hand Coven had had enough of its attic lair. It was a dim and draughty world that had very little in it apart from an awful lot of Welsh slate, Norwegian spruce timber beams and lashings of pigeon shit. With enough of its core cells re-grown it was time for it to slip out from the eaves, and escape to freedom down the soil vent pipe below the guttering brackets where it could acquire some new bacterial glue that wasn't derived exclusively from decomposing mice and bird droppings; then attend to the business of finding a suitable victim to finish the first stage of its regeneration. Someone who was a few pounds spare, or better still several stones ahead, of the needle-stop on their bathroom scales. Regenerative processes, in the case of supernatural entities, were very long and tedious unless the right kind of biological matter could be found to speed things up, and return the entity in question back to its proper proportions.

Occultists in the modern world just couldn't comprehend how many calories a demon burned up manifesting itself through the dense oscillating frequencies of short wave, medium wave and long wave radio waves; cluttering up the ether. Even without all the expanding and shrinking, doing evil burned up a lot of calories in the invisible world of broadcast signals and fax traces. Once it was drawn out of its lair on the lower planes of Hell, getting anywhere in a hurry since the birth of radio and television was like trying to sprint through a field of elephant grass. It was a miracle it had made it to the attic of the Dickens Hotel, from Cayton Bay, without manifesting the imprint of hundreds of television scripts on its DNA, or mixing up its otherworldly genes with John Peel's entire weekly playlist.

Once it was at the first soil pipe junction it divided, then split again, sending equal parts of its mass through the three branches of the exterior pipe into shorter interior connections, and thence up through the u-bends into the great unknown. Luckily, it emerged into the tainted water of the three ladies' toilet compartments without company, just as Maureen pushed open the door and moved toward the mirror. The demon hurriedly merged its separate parts at the top of the toilet cubicle frame and moved silently up the toilet wall. Tetarzepamdomestoz – now about the same size as a king size quilt cover and with the appearance of a filthy sheet of cellophane – rolled itself out across the ceiling to preserve its static charge, and then balled up over the first basin where its prey was attending to her right eye with the corner of a tissue.

Maureen Moment didn't have a clairvoyant "bone" in her body, or any particular aptitude for occult practices. But what she did have was a woman's natural sixth sense for trouble. As she was concentrating on flicking a stray eyelash from the corner of her eyeball she was suddenly gripped by a feeling that she was being watched by someone or something with malicious intent. The tiny hairs on the back of her neck became ramrod straight, and an icy chill began to ball between her shoulder blades. Then something that felt like a wet, mud-stained polytunnel cover fell onto her head and shoulders, and tried to wrap itself around her fatty neck. In the nick of time, Joy and Violet, buoyed up after half an hour of fresh air and two jugs of Perrier, staggered into the ladies', shrieking and cackling, just as their friend was about to lose consciousness and head-butt the edge of the sink. The sight of Maureen, staggering backwards and forwards, wreathed in a filthy cloud of flashing ectoplasm, must have had an immediate sobering effect of sorts on Violet in particular. Before Joy had uttered a word, her friend's talisman was spinning towards Maureen's head and shoulders like a stone from a sling.

'GET'OFF'ER-YA-FILTHY-BASTARD!' bellowed Violet, staggering towards the scene, of the possession gone wrong, like a drunken Dirty Harry; an atomiser raised like a gun at the glittering cloud of filthy vapour which had now let go of their sister witch and was choking on her talisman. 'GIMMIE YER OLEUM, JOY! QUICK!'

'GET DOWN, MO!' yelled Joy at Maureen who was already keeling over in a faint. Joy tossed Violet a small bottle which she caught with a confident swipe, presenting it to the demon that was folding in on itself and turning a queasy shade of purple.

'KNOW WHAT THIS IS DO YA – YA FILTHY BASTARD, bassterd... BACK OFF!' The dark cloud had shrunk to the size of a small pillowcase, and was making a sound like a recently cleared drain swallowing a backlog of dishwater, as it choked on Violet's engraved "Seal of Agrippa".

'GO GET THE BUGGER, VI!' screamed Joy, whooping with malice.

Violet flicked the cap off Joy's scent bottle, drew back her arm, and then threw the contents into the heart of what remained of Tetarzepamdomestoz; she fired off three long jets of holy water mixed with gin into the body of the smoke; it immediately changed into a spinning vortex and collapsed down to a malignant black spot in the air. There was a loud pop and then the spot fell to the floor as a small dark glass marble, and bounced harmlessly into the paper towel bin below the hand driers.

'Lord save us an' help us...' sighed Joy. 'That's enough excitement for one night, eh Vi? Nice work by the way, maid.'

'Give 'em an inch and they'll take a mile, demons.'

'Bassssterds...' muttered Violet. 'Get me to the sink, pet. I think I'm going to throw up.'

Violet tottered to the edge of the second hand basin and grabbed the two front corners to steady herself, bending forward towards the plughole.

'Start me off, Joy,' said Violet, bracing herself.

'D'you want me to get you round the waist, dear?'

'No, no, no... jusht shqueeze me tum... while I put me finger down me throat... thatch should do it.'

After a short abdominal convulsion three jets of something resembling minestrone soup, from the barrel of Violet's oesophagus, hit the bottom of the basin, firing her backwards into her friend's midriff, from which she bounced back onto the sink.

'Blumming 'eck, that's better,' she croaked, coughing coarsely like a heavy smoker. 'Get us a paper towel, Joy love.'

'Are you gonna lay on yer bloody back all night, Mo? Or are you coming back to the bar?' asked Vi, after wiping her chin with a paper towel.

'Maureen! What have you fallen in?' asked Derek, when the witches emerged from the ladies'.

'I haven't fallen into anything, *it fell on me.* Get me my coat, will you, and follow me upstairs… I need to get changed and take a shower.'

'Good God… is that that thing from Cayton Bay?'

'Yes, it damn well is! But don't worry yourself. Vi's gelded it with some gin and holy water. The rest of it's in the waste paper basket in the loos.'

'YOU CAN'T LEAVE A DEMON IN A WASTE PAPER BASKET!'

'SHUSH! There might be someone in these bedrooms.'

'Are you completely mad?'

'Fed up is what I am. Covered in goo and missing Chinese Presley. Your demon, by the way, is as harmless as one of our pre-paid envelopes. Violet turned it into a glass marble with her talisman.'

'Well, one of you is going to have to go back and find what's left of it so I can perform the banishing ritual.'

'I'm not putting my hand in basket of wet paper towels,

God only knows what else is in there. Can't we just leave it there and let it go to landfill?'

'No, we most certainly *can't*. As soon as Mars goes retrograde again, it'll start to regenerate if it's still in the open air. I'm going to have to take it to that Anchabadze woman on Landkey Island.'

'Sveta the Sorceress?'

'She's the only one who can make it safe until I can start another banishing ritual. I can't perform the ritual for another twenty-one days. There's no alignment. No-one else can make it safe in the meantime. I'm not over the moon about having to go over there, but there's no other way.'

'There's Robin the Druid.'

'I'm afraid Robin is more interested in where his next fix is coming from. He doesn't even leave his house these days for more than fifteen minutes. He's got more phobias than Howard Hughes. Robin is out of the picture. He's out of his bloody mind most of the time as well.'

'Which room are you in, Maureen?'

'I'm not in any bloody room, try some of the door handles.'

'But…'

'I can't clean myself up in the ladies, can I? I need to wash me hair and fix me face. If we can't find one unlocked on the first floor we'll try the second and the third. You can watch the door while I use one of the bathrooms.'

'What about your dress?'

'Oh that's all right, I had me mac on, I can rinse off the goo easily enough, if we can find a shower in here.'

Chapter Twenty-Six

The Love Policeman.

Whilst the Black Hand Coven were drinking the Dickens Hotel dry, Whitborough's finest detective double act were enjoying a few beers in the Leeds Arms.

'It's hard to know how this all fits together. It's a bloody mess is what it is,' moaned Broadhead.

'What I always do is start on the outside of the timeline and work in. I've bracketed the two weeks before the ship blew up and looked at all our cases, the unusual ones.'

'Dodds and Deighton's crash?'

'Mmmm.'

'What bothers me is the lack of detail from the statements around that incident at the Shirestones. I told you how strange that interview we did with the chef was, not so long ago, didn't I? People aren't generally that guarded during an interview. It reminded me of a case I was trying to break a few years ago; a local slum landlord that we were certain we had the evidence to get him on extortion and fraud. But when it came to the trial, no-one would testify. They'd all been got at – or bought. The only difference here is the suspect wasn't human, and I can't shake the feeling it wasn't an animal either – not the kind people are familiar with anyway. God, this case is a headache…'

'What was the name of Boldwood's youngest staff member?'

'Billy Sharpe. His mother's going to want to bring him in and sit out the interview.'

'Fair enough. As long as she keeps her trap shut.'

'You know he's got Down's syndrome, Ray?'

'Oh he'll be all right, George. We might actually find out more from him than we will from talking to anyone else. It doesn't mean he's any less capable than you or me.'

'Right, I'll get him in.'

'What's the other one called?'

'Ben Wilson. Rides a motorbike. Headbanger.'

'Mmm, I know the sort.'

'He's doing his A Levels, at the sixth form college.'

'Is he now?'

'You want them in back to back?'

'Yep. We'll quiz Billy first. Have one in the suite, one on the seats. Just so they see each other coming in and out.'

'No-one in the frame for the missing donkeys yet?'

'I've got Fu on it. He's found a footprint on Whapple Bank and a couple of broken bangles with some coloured string behind a park bench. One of the lads from the Air Cadets rang the station to say they saw two punks; a really tall lad with two donkeys, and a young woman in an old RAF greatcoat, with blue hair, in the top of their paddock, behind the hedge. Could be that lot from Burniston…'

'There must be hundreds of punks in Whitborough, guv.'

'Yes, but I'll bet there aren't that many who'd contemplate stealing a stableful of donkeys… whose stable is that?'

'Val Metcalfe's…' said Broadhead, with a look of reverence.

'Manshipp's Val Metcalfe?'

'Yep. The one and only.'

'Well, God help 'em when she finds out they've nicked her mules.'

'God help the poor bastards who've nicked Ted Knight's Merc.'

Chapter Twenty-Seven

I Want Cheese.

At ten o'clock on the second day of Inspector Marshall's "return to duty" he conducted an interview with Billy Sharpe, Lindsay Boldwood's most junior staff member, and his mother, in the ground-floor interview suite. In the room were Sergeant Broadhead, seated beside Marshall, and Constable Elland at attention by the door.

'Now Billy, we understand that you've been helping your Uncle Lindsay, the landlord at the Shirestones Hotel in Cloughton, for your work experience for school. Detective Sergeant Broadhead and I would like to ask you a few questions. You're not in any trouble, Billy. We'd just like to know if you've witnessed – pardon me – *if you've seen* anything bad happen while you were working there,' said Marshall, correcting himself under the disapproving gaze of Billy's mother.

'Bad fings?'

'Yes, bad things – like people fighting – or people hiding animals indoors. Wolves, for example.'

'What kind of fool brings a wolf back to their bedsit, Inspector?'

'Students, Mrs Sharpe. You wouldn't believe the things they get up to. I had a half-eaten doner kebab stuffed in my car's front grille, and a rude message in mayonnaise on my windscreen, last time we had rag week. If you'd like me to repeat anything, Billy, then just say so. This won't take long and then you can go home with your mum – all right?'

'Yeth.'

'Is there anything you'd like to drink… a cup of tea or coffee, whilst you're thinking?'

'Billy doesn't like hot drinks, Inspector. He only drinks squash or water.'

'We've got Vimto. Would you like some Vimto, Billy… we could make it exactly how you like it?'

'I want *cheese*…'

'They don't have any cheese, Billy.'

'Go and get the lad some Vimto from the canteen, Elland.'

'In a glass, sir?'

'No – *in a vase* – you plonker!'

'Sorry, Inspector, Billy's not being funny. He always asks for cheese when he gets anxious. He doesn't mean anything by it; it's just his *safe word*. You don't have to worry about what you say, Billy. Just tell these gentlemen what you know and then we can all go home.'

'His *safe word*… right – okay. Well Billy… There's no reason that you should feel anxious with us, is there, George?' said Marshall, omitting his colleague's title in the hope of creating a friendlier, less formal atmosphere in the interview suite.

'Nobody is going to make you say something you don't want to say. We just want you to tell us things that we might not know. Things *you might know*. We need your help, you see, Billy. We can't do anything without you, because what you know is very important, you see. And we need you to tell us what you've seen at the Shirestones while you've been working there for Uncle Lindsay,' he said, winking at Mrs Sharpe. 'Would you like to tell us who you saw smashing down the back door at the Shirestones?'

'It was werewolf. Me and my fwend saw werewolf once in Silver Street Picture House. With Dra-cala and Flanken-stin.'

'A werewolf?' It wasn't a bear?'

'Werewolves can't be bears. I know. I know coz I seen bears in books. Bears eat salmon. I like chee…'

'Cheese, yes Billy… Are you sure it wasn't a big dog, Billy?'

'It was werewolf. How can werewolf be dog?'

'George?'

'Guv?'

'Would you like to ask Billy a question, George?'

'Werewolves aren't real, Billy.'

'I want *cheese…*'

'I think that's all you're going to get from Billy now, gentlemen. Two or three questions in succession are his limit; once he starts to feel anxious, you're wasting your time, he'll just keep asking for cheese.'

'I want *cheese.*'

'Have some Vimto, Billy.'

'I want to go to my room now.'

'Later, Billy,' said his mother, sympathetically, 'soon.'

'We need to wait for his anxieties to fade for a few minutes. Have you got anything he can draw on? He quite likes to scribble when he's winding down before bed. Would you like to draw the werewolf, Billy?'

'Might do…'

'For fish – chips?'

'An' mush – peas?'

'And mush – peas.'

'An' thauce?'

'And th… sauce.'

'I know…'

'Well done, Billy.'

When the interview was over Broadhead escorted Billy out of the interview room with PC Elland, whilst Marshall thanked his mother.

'I don't think we'll be able to use Billy's testimony, Mrs Sharpe. He's obviously trying to cover up something to protect somebody he knows. Whether we'll ever get him to tell the truth, I don't know.'

'What he's told you is the truth, as far as he's concerned.'

'Pardon?'

'Billy can't lie, Inspector. He couldn't tell a lie or construct one. He doesn't have that capacity. He can only tell the truth, or the truth as he sees it.'

'Thank you, Mrs Sharpe. George will see you both out.'

'Don't you want him to write a statement?'

'By all means, I just don't want to put my name to it…'

Chapter Twenty-Eight

Black Magic Woman.

At daybreak the lazy morning sun began its slow arc into a patchy blue sky dominated by gathering thunder clouds. Derek Beautimann arrived in the cliff top car park, at the farthest end of Compass Rose Lane – on the northernmost edge of Whitborough, in his Jaguar. Opening his door, he swung his legs out onto the verge and changed his shoes for a pair of green Wellington boots, then stood up, pulled on his Barbour jacket and put on his cap; locking his car before setting off towards the footpath leading down the face of Scalby Beck Cliffs above the high shale banks and sandbars. The sea was glassy calm as the tide retreated slowly back to the reef, exposing Landkey causeway – a giant snake with glittering scales stretching out to the great rock island four miles away. In thirty minutes the whole length of the limestone pavement would be clear of the sea; and the great kelp beds and mats of bladderwrack would start to release their salty aroma as the gulls descended onto the rock pools, looking for fish and crustaceans. The bulk of Landkey was usually hidden in the morning mists; though the great mirror of the lighthouse would continue to revolve until the clouds lifted or were burnt off by the sun.

Few people used the causeway to reach Landkey after the Dellingpole Ferry service was set up in 1930. The great rock pavement was treacherously slippery, unless the sun had baked the algae and seaweed dry at low tide, and the air teemed with seabirds relieving themselves on the wing. But Derek could not risk being recognised taking the boat, so he had no other option if he wanted to get to his appointment at Weareburgh and remain incognito. There would be no time to linger, or admire the views. With the causeway still wet he would have to watch his footing, and follow the driest line through the seagrass, if he hoped to stay upright during his walk across the bay.

Sveta Anchabadze, the sorceress of Landkey Island, was the youngest granddaughter of Count Nikolai Anchabadze, a member of an old aristocratic Russian family. Her grandfather had purchased Weareburgh as an insurance policy, after temporarily re-locating his family to safety in Königsberg, during the Russian revolution. The Anchabadze family escaped the Soviets, but lost their most productive and entrepreneurial members to the influenza pandemic of 1919.

Weareburgh was declared contaminated and was sealed up. Sveta's two remaining sisters found work as nurses, but Sveta, a gifted clairvoyant, was harried by the spirits of her dead relatives, and eventually delivered into an asylum by her treacherous step-mother, from which she managed to escape by changing places with her deceased cellmate. Once in the morgue she had cut herself out of the heavy linen sack and escaped through an open window. She then returned to Weareburgh to live as a semi-recluse.

Sveta conducted her magical rituals in a round tower, connected south of the main house, which was accessed by an underground passage from the cellars of Weareburgh. The roof of the tower had been designed as a gun platform;

copying the pattern of the once plentiful Martello Towers on the south coast. It had three floors: a basement magazine, an open plan accommodation block and kitchen, and a second floor observation room with a line of six windows at intervals of thirty degrees overlooking the coast and headland. It was this room that Sveta used for her magical practice, to take advantage of the inlaid brass compass points and circular border milled into the wooden plank floor.

Derek's brisk walk to Landkey took him the best part of an hour. He decided to visit the Briny Ewe for a couple of fortifying gin and tonics, to steady his nerves, before setting off along the coastal path to Weareburgh; Sveta had always made him feel ill at ease. Despite their history, she was an even greater mystery to him after their brief liaison than she had been before. Their short relationship had been a clash of personalities and cultures as volatile and contradictory as could be imagined, as exasperating and tiring as it was destructive. They had been fortunate to fall out and go their separate ways before one of them had got too tired of the other.

'You should visit us more often.'

'Us? I thought you were alone, Sveta?'

'My family is always present here. On edge of sight. They help me with my works.'

'Your works?'

'It is not like your works. I lay ground for many lifelines – and fates. I do not invite devils here.'

'I don't consort with devils just for the hell of it.'

'No, for you is money, Derek. Always for money. You should be careful to balance… is not to say I cannot help you with your dickavent.'

'Predicament…'

'Predickavent. Yes. The demon that brought you here. He is behind glass? But not banished?'

'Yes, how did you know?'

'I sense him. It is why you are here – no?'

'I need this thing neutralised. Until Monday week. I can deal with it afterwards on my own.'

'So confident, as always.'

'Will you help?'

'Of course. You know my price.'

'Could I not just give you money, Sveta?'

'No. I am not prostitute… Roll up sleeve…'

'That kn…knife of yours is clean… isn't it?'

'You do not think my spit is clean?'

'OH GOD…'

'Hold hand in fist now over cup.'

'How much of my blood are you going to take? I've got to walk back over the causeway – I can't walk back through all the seaweed feeling dizzy.'

'I have much tea, spirits, to make up your fluids… other things?'

'I'll have some tea please.'

'Dandelion – or nettle?'

'What's your wine made from?'

'No wine. Wine is drink for Western woman. I have Polinka, Polinka is better… you try before?'

'Can I just have some water?'

'Yes. I have to get from barrel. You want now or after?'

'Barrel?'

'Yes… rainwater barrel.'

'Perhaps I'll have some dandelion tea…'

'Hold out your hand now.'

'OWWW!' cried Derek, as Sveta made a long swift cut across his left palm, grinning with satisfaction as he proceeded to bleed all over the cup and his Hunter Wellington boots.

'Ahhh… Blood is good… strong! You bleed, till I tell you stop. Yes? Hold knife…'

'Me?'

'Yes – with other hand that is not bled… I swap cups, lead cup first, silver cup now.'

'Oh God…' moaned Derek resentfully. 'Did you really have to cut me that deeply? How on Earth is it going to heal before I have to go back to work? I can't turn up on Monday morning at work with my hand swathed in bandages, it doesn't look very professional.'

'Is no deep, you are big baby.'

'It HURTS.'

'I give you special salve to cover cut. Heal very quick. By Monday – no bandage you will see. Keep hand still.'

'When can I go, Sveta?'

'You stay until midnight.'

'What!'

'Demon is tied to you. Spell I must make must be after nine o'clock. You must be in inner circle during blessing or all for nothing. Go home tomorrow!'

'But I hadn't arranged to…'

'No argue. You will have room in tower. Make up fire with logs in bunker. You wish to shave in morning?'

'I haven't got a…'

'No worry. I fix. I have Bic.'

'You have Bic razors?'

183

'Yes. Good for legs! Only use mirror on wall, not mirror on window sill. Wrap in sack, before dawn, put in drawer.'

'I shan't ask why.'

'No secret – is magic mirror.'

'You are hungry?'

'Well, I have lobster and seaweed, with bread I make.'

'Seaweed?'

'Yes, very good – good for blood. Good for you… I steam with lobster.'

'You're too kind…'

Chapter Twenty-Nine

White Rabbit.

A light-blue unmarked Ford Escort saloon, containing a smart young oriental gentleman in plain clothes, and a thrusting young blonde lady with a business-like shoulder bag, drew up into the lecturer's parking bay at Whitborough Technical College. The couple were seen to converse for a few minutes by the groundsman who had stopped to rebuke the visitors for parking in a space reserved for staff. When they eventually extracted themselves from their car, and prepared to move off, he decided it was time to make them aware of their error.

'Can't park there…'

'And who are you?' asked the man in the smart mac.

'I'm the man who's telling you you can't park there. It's reserved for lecturers, that is, an' the board o' governors. Can't park there.'

'We're the police,' said Detective Constable Fu, holding out his warrant card.

'Well I suppose that'll be all right, for a while…'

'Where is the Art and Design department, please?' asked DC Fu coldly.

'Up the steps, past reception, left at the end of the corridor and over the bridge.'

'Thank you for your co-operation,' said Fu, bringing their short exchange to a halt.

'I'll be sodding off then,' muttered the groundsman to himself as he turned away to pick up some more litter.

'Charming man,' commented his partner, DC Spencer, lighting up her cigarette. 'Do you want one, Fu?'

'I don't smoke,' he replied.

'Please yourself.'

'We go and talk to this girl now. Okay?'

'Can I finish me fag first?'

'No.'

'You wouldn't let me have one in the car.'

'Because smoking bad for you. Your smoke – is bad for me.'

'Blimey, I'm only having one. Anyway... what if this girl's in an exam or something?'

'End of exam.'

'Shouldn't we wait?'

'Wait?'

'But it could be embarassing...'

'For who?'

'For *her.*'

'All citizens of United Kingdom under law. Including students in exam or not.'

'Oh, for goodness sake!'

'If she not co-operate, she come with us. No if or but. Is way we do in Hong Kong.'

'No ifs or buts.'

'You got that right!'

'Mary Shipley Browne...' said Spencer, reading aloud from her notebook, 'student activist and agitator. Sounds like a right bitch.'

Mary was just coming out of her hallucinogenic odyssey, back from her terrifying encounter with Val Metcalfe, and hidden in the womb of a pile of stale beanbags when Fu and Spencer found her.

'Mary Shipley Browne?'

'Yeah. That's me. Who are you?'

'Detective Constable Fu – to you, Miss.'

'Oh yeaaah… whaaa d'you want,' she mumbled, slurring.

'Mary Shipley Browne, I'm arresting you for breaking and entering, damage to private property, the theft, abduction and abandonment of several valuable, privately owned animals, the illegal dumping of a motor vehicle, fly-tipping and allowing an animal to foul a public footpath…'

'FASCIST! Ain't done nuffing – nuffing – nuffing.'

'Have you been drinking – Miss Browne?'

'DRINKING? DRINKING! You can't even get a shandy in 'ere.'

'You are intoxicated, Miss Browne.'

'I ain't intoc… intox… ox-icrated… I'm tri… tripping.'

'Do you require medical attention before we take you to the police station?'

'Medicinal?'

'MED–I–CAL.'

'What?'

'You're swaying, Miss Browne – and your pupils are dilated – and you're dribbling from the corner of your mouth. Would you like a tissue?'

'No – yeah… WOT?'

'Do you have a child with you?'

'EH?'

'You are in the nursery, Miss Browne.'

'I only come in here to hide, cos it's closed this afternoon. I felt ill so I came in to chill out and get away from everyone else. You gonna arrest me?'

'Yes. You are under arrest, Miss Browne.'

'I ain't going anywhere until I speak to him…'

'Who?' asked Fu, turning around to see who their prisoner was pointing at.

'Him – with the scruffy trousers an' the trilby,' said Mary, staring unsteadily at Inspector Marshall as he made his way across the car park, 'my dad's mate.'

Once Mary had been settled into the back of Marshall's Ford Escort, with the other two members of his team following behind, the party set off for Whitborough Police Station.

'What's that awful smell? Something in here smells like a skip full of sweaty sports kits,' said Marshall, grimacing.

'It's her in the back, Guv, she's rank,' said DC Spencer, wrinkling her nose.

'I beg your pardon!' screeched Mary. 'My hair is not rank, that's the smell of sebum and natural oils.'

'No offence, Mary, but you should get that hair of yours washed before you go out in public – I think we'd better have the windows down, Spencer.'

'How dare you! I want to speak with my solicitor… now!'

'Is he in Burniston, Miss Browne?'

'I've never used one!'

'I find that hard to believe…'

'What did you say?'

'Would you like to use the duty solicitor at the station – I should warn you he does have a functioning sense of smell.'

'I want to speak to my father.'

'Instead of the duty solicitor? You're entitled to make one phone call, Miss.'

'I want to call my dad.'

'You may. But we have to get to the station first. And we will be driving with the windows down.'

'You're all *fascists*!'

'No, Miss, we're police officers and we have a very normal aversion to bad smells. Now be quiet, or you'll be going to the station in the dog-section transport with Fredo and Vito, and I'll tell your dad you've resisted my arresting officer.'

Just after setting off with the dribbling Queen of the Underground, Marshall got a radio call from the station.

'Priority call, all cars, burnt-out Mercedes Saloon found at Filey Lakes picnic ground, over. Please respond.'

'I've got it, Trudy,' replied Marshall.

'Are we taking her?' asked Broadhead.

'Yes, we are – she can sit still and shut up!'

Chapter Thirty

The Banishing.

In the observatory wing of the Martello Tower on Weareburgh, Derek Beautimann awoke, to find his legs and arms tied to four iron rings set into the stone floor, in the centre of a number of chalk rings topped with salt. His host, dressed in a white hooded gown with long sleeves, ignored his return to consciousness, and continued with her invocations, drawing strange and wondrous shapes in the air with her hazel wand.

Derek wondered what it was about the occasion that required him to be stripped naked, and couldn't resist the thought that his host was a frustrated sex maniac as well as an unhinged sorceress with a fetish for bloodletting, stinging nettle poultice and sea bathing. His trip to Landkey was turning into a personal endurance test. The pesto and curry sauce stains on the loaned copy of his first edition *De Occulta Philosophia* now seemed to be quite unimportant. Tetarzepamdomestoz, demon lord of mines, caves and underground places, was resting in an iron dish on his abdomen in its glass marble prison. Suddenly there seemed to be an awful lot of smoke pouring into the chamber from the lift shaft indent by the wall. Sveta, still engrossed in her preparations, then began to reinforce their outer circle with more salt. Returning to the centre of the room, she opened a bottle of gin from the altar and took a huge swig. Then turned to Derek and grinned.

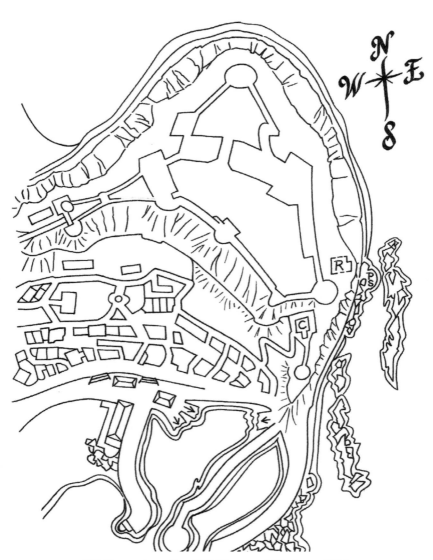

Whitborough on Sea Old Town and Harbour, 1983

Whitborough on Sea

Principal street index